THE SWORD THIEF

PETER LERANGIS

SCHOLASTIC INC.

NEW YORK   TORONTO   LONDON   AUCKLAND
SYDNEY   MEXICO CITY   NEW DELHI   HONG KONG

Scholastic Children's Books
An imprint of Scholastic Ltd
Euston House, 24 Eversholt Street
London, NW1 1DB, UK
Registered office: Westfield Road, Southam, Warwickshire, CV47 0RA
SCHOLASTIC and associated logos are trademarks
and/or registered trademarks of Scholastic Inc.

First published in the US by Scholastic Inc, 2009
This edition published in the UK by Scholastic Ltd, 2012

Text copyright © Scholastic Inc, 2009

Book design and illustration by SJI Associates, Inc.

The right of Peter Lerangis to be identified as the author
of this work has been asserted by him.

ISBN 978 1407 13562 5

Printed and bound by CPI Group (UK) Ltd, Croydon, CR0 4YY
Papers used by Scholastic Children's Books are made from wood
grown in sustainable forests.

5 7 9 10 8 6 4

www.scholastic.co.uk/zone

For Tina, Nick, and Joe, always.

— PL

CHAPTER 1

They were toast.

Amy Cahill eyed the battered black duffel bag rumbling up the airport conveyor belt. It bulged at the corners. The sign above the belt said THANK YOU FOR VISITING VENICE: RANDOM PIECES OF CHECKED LUGGAGE WILL BE SEARCHED in five languages.

"Oh, great," Amy said. "How random is 'random'?"

"I told you, a ninja warrior must always keep his swords in his carry-on," whispered her brother, Dan, who had been operating on brain deficit for as long as Amy could remember.

"Excuse me, Jackie Chan, but carry-on luggage is *always* X-rayed," Amy whispered back. "There are extra-special rules about samurai swords in *backpacks*. Even if they belong to scrawny, delusional eleven-year-olds who think they're ninjas."

"What was wrong with 'we need them to slice the veal parmigiana'?" Dan said. "It would have worked fine. The Italians understand food."

"Can *you* understand 'five to twenty years, no parole'?"

Dan shrugged. He lifted up a mesh-sided pet carrier, inside of which a very disgruntled-looking Egyptian Mau was eyeing him suspiciously. "Bye-bye, Saladin," he sang into the mesh. "Remember, when we get to Tokyo . . . red snapper sushi every night!"

"Mrrp?" whined Saladin from inside the carrier, as Dan set it gently onto the conveyor belt.

"Mmmm, hmm, ohh . . . *aaaaaaaaghhhh*!" came a strangled yelp from behind them. Although everyone else in the vicinity was turning with a look of alarm, Amy and Dan knew it was their au pair, Nellie Gomez, dancing to a tune on her iPod. She didn't care that she sounded like a dying meerkat, which was one of the many cool things about Nellie Gomez.

Amy watched as the carrier disappeared through the cargo window. If the officials did search the bag, there would be alarms. Screaming Italian cops. She, Dan, and Nellie would have to run.

Not that they weren't used to that. They'd been running a lot lately. It began the day they accepted the challenge in their grandmother Grace's will. They'd had to go to her mansion in Massachusetts for that — and immediately afterward the mansion went up in flames. Since then, they'd nearly been killed in a collapsing building in Philadelphia, attacked by monks in Austria, and chased by boats through the canals of Venice. They'd been the target of dirty tricks from every branch of the Cahill family.

Once in a while—like every three seconds—Amy wondered why the heck they were doing this. She and Dan could have opted for a cool million dollars each, like a lot of Cahill family members did. But Grace had offered another choice: a race for 39 Clues to a secret that had been hidden for centuries, the greatest source of power the world had known.

Until then, Amy and Dan had been leading pretty lame, ordinary lives. After their parents had died seven years ago, their crabby Aunt Beatrice had taken them in—and the only cool thing she'd ever done was hire Nellie. But now they knew they were part of something way bigger, a huge family that included ancestors like Ben Franklin and Wolfgang Amadeus Mozart. It seemed like all the great geniuses of the world had been Cahills. That was pretty amazing.

"Hey, Amy, did you ever want to, like, get on the conveyor belt and see what happened? Like, 'Hey, don't mind me, I'm just hanging with the cargo'?"

And then there was Dan.

"Come on!" Amy grabbed her brother by the arm and headed for the departure gates. Nellie was right on their heels, spinning the wheel of her iPod with one hand and adjusting her snake nose ring with the other.

Amy eyed the airport clock. 2:13. The flight was scheduled to leave at 2:37. This was an international flight. You were supposed to arrive at the airport *two hours* in advance, not twenty-four minutes. "We're not going to make it!" Amy said.

Now they were running toward gate 4, dodging other passengers. "Guess they didn't find Rufus and Remus, huh?" Dan called out.

"Who are Rufus and Remus?" Amy asked.

"The swords!" Dan said. "I named them after the founders of Italy."

"It's *Romulus* and Remus," Amy hissed. "And they founded Rome. And don't *ever* say that word!"

"Rome?"

"No — s-w-o-r-d." Amy dropped her voice to a whisper as they pulled up to the rear of a very long security line. "Do you want us to go to *j-a-i-l*?"

"O-o-p-s."

"O-O-O-O . . . " Nellie wailed off-key to some unidentifiable punk track.

The security line seemed to take, like, thirty-two hours. The worst part for Amy, as always, was having to take off her jade necklace to go through the X-ray machine. She hated to part from that necklace even for a minute. When they emerged, the clock read 2:31. They raced down a long corridor toward the gate.

"Now boarding all remaining passengers for Japan Airlines, flight eight-oh-seven to Tokyo, at gate four," said a voice over the PA system in heavily accented English. "Have your boarding passes ready, and . . . *arrrrrrrivederci!*"

They pulled up to the rear of the line behind a sniffling toddler who turned and sneezed on Nellie. "Ew. Manners?" she said, wiping her arm on her sleeve.

"Has anyone seen my boarding pass?" Dan said, rummaging in his pockets.

"Have mine," drawled Nellie. "It's covered with boogers."

"Try inside your book," Amy said, pointing toward the paperback stuffed in Dan's back pants pocket.

He pulled out a dog-eared copy of *Classic All-Time Movie Comedies*, which he'd found in the backseat of the cab on the way to the airport. The boarding pass was marking page 93. "*It's a Mad, Mad, Mad, Mad World*," Dan said.

"That's the smartest observation you've made all day," Amy said.

"It's the name of a movie," Dan replied. "I'm reading about it. The plot is so awesome—"

"Step forward, please—welcome aboard!" chirped a perky blond flight attendant whose Japan Airlines headset bobbed every time she nodded a greeting. She was wearing a name tag that read I. RINALDI.

Nellie handed over her boarding pass and headed into the accordion-walled tunnel that led to the plane's hatch. "Um, guys, this shouldn't be so hard to do," she called over her shoulder.

Dan held out his pass to the attendant. "It's really a funny movie. Like, all these old-school comedians, searching for this treasure—"

"Sorry, he's challenged," Amy said to the attendant, handing over her pass and nudging him toward the tunnel.

But Ms. Rinaldi scooted in front of them, blocking their path. *"Un momento?"* she said, trying to keep her airline smile while listening to something over her headset. *"Sì . . . ah, sì sì sì sì . . . buono,"* she said into the headset mike.

Then, with a shrug toward Dan and Amy, she said, "You come with me, please?"

As they followed her toward the corner, Amy tried to keep herself from shaking. The swords. They'd found the swords.

Dan was looking all puppy-eyed at her. Sometimes all she needed to do was look at him, and she knew exactly what he was thinking.

Maybe we should run, his eyes were saying.

Uh, where? she said back to him silently.

I will make myself invisible by using ninja mind control, he was thinking.

You have to HAVE a mind to do it, she beamed to him.

Nellie peered out from the tunnel entrance. "What's going on?" she asked.

"It is routine," Ms. Rinaldi called out, turning to face Amy and Dan. "My supervisor tells me it is random check. You please wait here by the wall?"

She bustled away, holding the two boarding passes, and disappeared around the corner.

From inside the tunnel, another attendant called out to Nellie, "Please take your seat, dear. Don't worry, the plane will not leave without all passengers."

"I hate airports." Nellie rolled her eyes and turned back toward the plane. "See you inside. I'll save you a bag of peanuts."

As she disappeared, Amy hissed to her brother, "I knew it—they searched your duffel. They're going to detain us and contact Aunt Beatrice, and that's the last we'll ever see of Nellie —"

"Will you stop being so gloomy?" Dan said. "We'll tell them someone else put the swor—the you-know-whats in the duffel. We never saw them before in our lives. We're kids. They always believe kids. And besides, maybe they *haven't* searched our bags. Maybe they're just double-checking your passport to make sure they can allow someone so ugly to board a plane—"

Amy elbowed him in the ribs.

"Final boarding call, flight eight-oh-seven to Tokyo, gate four!" a voice boomed.

A third attendant was putting a web-ribbon barrier in front of the tunnel.

Amy was nervous now. They weren't going to hold the plane forever. "We have to get that flight attendant—Rinaldi," she said. "Come on!"

Amy grabbed Dan by the arm and they raced to the corner, taking it at a run.

Whomp! They ran smack into another pair who were racing toward the gate. Amy bounced away, the wind momentarily knocked out of her. She bumped into Dan, who nearly fell to the floor. "What the—?" he blurted.

The two strangers were wrapped in full-length black trench coats with high collars obscuring their faces. One of them wore expensive black dress shoes; the other, jewel-encrusted sneakers. As they barreled past Dan and Amy, waving boarding passes in the air, one of them called out, "Clear, please!"

Amy recognized the voice. She grabbed Dan and whirled around. The two were grabbing the barrier and pulling it aside. "Wait!" Amy said.

An airline official shouted at them, too, sprinting to head them off. The two politely stopped and handed over their boarding passes. He examined the passes quickly, nodded, and pulled back the barrier. "Enjoy your flight, Amy and Dan," he said.

The two passengers stepped into the tunnel entrance and immediately turned around. They pulled down their raised collars and grinned.

Amy gasped at the sight of their cousins, their archrivals in the search for the 39 Clues, a pair whose nastiness was surpassed only by their wealth and cunning.

"*Sayonara,* suckers!" sang Ian and Natalie Kabra.

CHAPTER 2

"*Stop them!*" Dan and Amy ran toward the tunnel, shouting as loud as they could.

Quickly, the flight official stepped into their path. "Boarding passes, *per favore*?" he asked, his face a mix of bafflement and annoyance.

Amy watched helplessly as Ian and Natalie slipped into the tunnel's long shadow.

They could hear the plane's hatch shut with a dull *thump*.

"They're—they're the Kabras!" Dan said. "Evil Kabras. *Famoso, evillo, Kabritos!* They are holding our au pair hostage!"

As a crowd of curious onlookers gathered, the official repeated, "No boarding passes?"

He was looking straight at Amy. Dan glanced frantically her way, his eyes screaming, *You're the older one—do something!*

The thoughts were firing around in Amy's brain like a broken laser-light show. How could the Kabras be here? She and Dan had left them unconscious in a smoldering room in Venice. Who had rescued them? How had they recovered so fast? How had they stolen the tickets?

Everyone was looking at Amy now. The whole airport. She hated when people stared at her. She hated it even worse when it involved being humiliated by the Kabras. They were always one step ahead, always one Clue closer to the Cahill secret. No matter how hard Amy and Dan tried, the Kabras were smarter, faster, cooler—and ruthless. They were impersonating Dan and Amy. They were about to ambush a defenseless au pair. How could Amy possibly communicate all this? She opened her mouth to try, but it was too much. Too many eyes. She felt as if someone had tied off her vocal cords. Nothing came out.

"Ohhh-*kay,* thank you, Amy," Dan said. "Um, look, dude—officer—these guys? The Kabras? Well, actually, they're a guy and a girl? They ripped us off, okay? *Comprendo?* The tickets say Cahill and they're not Cahills—well, technically they are, but it's a different branch of the family, they're like Janus, I mean *Lucians,* and we don't know what we are, I mean what *branch,* but we're related—anyway, we're all kind of involved in something, sort of this battle about our grandmother's will, you could say, but it's kind of a long story and *THEY HAVE TO BE STOPPED! PRONTO!*"

"Sorry," the official said, "if you have no boarding—"

Amy grabbed Dan by the arm. This wasn't getting

them anywhere. They needed to find Ms. Rinaldi — or the supervisor who had summoned her. That person would rank higher than anyone here. Maybe there was still a chance. Maybe they could stop the plane from taking off.

She and Dan ran toward the corner again and rounded it. They raced past the place where they had collided with the Kabras, and immediately they emerged into the main corridor. In the distance they could see a line of shops. To their right was a supply closet and a glass door marked AUTHORIZED PERSONNEL ONLY.

To their left, a knot of onlookers surrounded the entrance to the women's room, where a group of EMT workers emerged, carrying a woman on a stretcher. Police were running in to join them from all directions.

Chaos. Total pandemonium. Amy strained to see around the rush of people as she ran, hoping to find a familiar face.

There.

A flash of blond hair, tossed over a shoulder, drew Amy's eyes to the right. "Dan, look!"

"Oh, *now* you can talk," Dan said. "What?"

Winding swiftly through the crowd was a tall woman in a Japan Airlines uniform about a size too large.

The sight of the familiar figure was enough to unlock Amy's loudest outdoor voice. *"IRINA!"* she blurted out.

There was no mistaking Irina Spasky—the stiff military bearing, the bladelike motion of the shoulders as she walked. Irina was another of the Cahill family bent on finding the 39 Clues. Like Ian and Natalie, she was ruthless. Unlike Ian and Natalie, she had been trained in espionage by the KGB.

Irina did not turn. She showed no outward signs of hearing Amy, aside from a quickening of her step.

Then she disappeared into the throng as if she'd never been there.

"Stop her!" Dan sprinted forward, nearly colliding with a rather sour-looking man in a wheelchair.

"Polizia!" the man shouted, lifting his cane as if to whack Dan over the head.

Dan ducked. Amy pulled him away, trying to keep an eye on Irina. They plowed forward, elbowing their way around passengers.

When they emerged into a less crowded area near the end of the terminal, Irina was nowhere to be seen. "She's gone," Dan said.

"I—I don't believe this," Amy said, catching her breath. "She was working with Ian and Natalie. They sabotaged us *together.*"

"Are we *sure* that was her?" Dan asked. "I mean, how would Irina manage to get that uniform?"

Before he finished the question, a voice shouted in Italian over a bullhorn, and the crowd quickly parted. A small ambulance made its way through the airport, siren blaring.

Murmurs were passing through the crowd, mostly in languages Amy didn't understand. But she spotted a couple with sunglasses, lots of cameras, awful Hawaiian shirts, and vapid smiles. "Look, Dan—Americans," she said. "Let's listen. . . . "

They both wandered closer until they could hear snatches of conversation. The people were talking about the woman on the stretcher.

Dan looked confused. "She was salted in the ladies' room?"

"*Assaulted,*" Amy said. "She must have been the flight supervisor, Dan! Irina knocked her out and took her uniform."

"Wow," Dan replied, looking almost impressed.

Amy glanced toward the window, where she saw the jet slowly backing away from gate 4 and onto the tarmac.

They were leaving. Detached from the tunnel, taxiing for the runway.

Amy panicked. "Don't look now, but they're going!"

"Where's the door? We can still run after them!"

"Right. You do that, Dan. Meanwhile I'll try to talk my way onto the next flight—a ticket for *one,* while they're scraping your remains out of the jet engine that sucked you in." Amy began running again, back toward the reservation desk. "Or you can come with me!"

Outside, the windows of flight 807 were dull silver-black holes in the distance. Amy knew that behind one of them was Nellie, in a situation no human being should ever have to face.

She was alone with the Kabras.

* * *

Dan followed Amy past the crowded security checkpoint, back toward the reception desk. The line for tickets doubled around at least three times, and they took their places at the back.

They exchanged a silent glance. Amy knew Dan was thinking exactly the same thing she was. He sighed, his saddened eyes wandering slowly to the conveyor belt. "Saladin's on the plane, too," Dan said. "And our swords."

Amy fought the urge to just collapse and cry. Right there in the middle of the terminal. Everything was going wrong. It had been a seven-year string of bad luck, ever since their parents died in that house fire. How were Amy and Dan supposed to do this alone? The Kabras had money. Their parents supported them. Plus, they were working with Irina. The Holts were a whole family. Jonah Wizard had his dad planning every moment of his life. It was Amy and Dan against . . . families. Teams. Generations. They didn't stand a chance.

If only Grace had told them earlier, back when their mom and dad had been alive. If only they were alive now! Thinking about them just made Amy feel worse. She'd been dreaming about them every night. She'd see their faces at odd times — smiling, confident, kind. She could sense their approval or disapproval, their pride whenever she got things right. They'd be there in her mind and then — *whoosh!* Gone. And she'd feel the loss all over.

"Amy?" Dan said quizzically. And there they were — *again*. In the eyes of El Dweebo. Not their faces, exactly, but *them*. Looking out at her, as if they'd just borrowed Dan's features for a moment. Which no other sane person would do.

In that moment, she knew exactly what the right decision was.

"There's a flight leaving at five-ten," she said, reading the overhead departures screen. "Nellie's safety is at stake. We have to follow."

"Hey, coolio — no retreat, *no surrender*!" Dan whooped. "So. Any thoughts about how we're going to pay for it?"

WAWWP! WAWWP! WAWWP! WAWWP!

An alarm rocked the terminal, stopping all conversation. As a terse announcement resounded, first in Italian, then French, then German, sections of the crowd began heading for the entrance — until finally:

"Ladies and gentlemen, please proceed immediately to the nearest exit, as this terminal must be evacuated for safety reasons. . . ."

A scream ripped the air, and then people were rushing, falling over one another. Amy ran toward the door, pulling her brother behind her, listening to shouted fragments around them, some of them in English:

"Bomb scare . . . "

"Terrorists . . . "

"Anonymous phone call . . . "

They reached the door and pushed their way through. The day had turned gray, but the winding access roads were dotted with the headlights of approaching vehicles. Passengers crowded the sidewalk, shouting into cell phones, hurtling toward buses and cabs. Dan and Amy pushed against the crush of bodies toward the curb, where the last of a group had climbed onto a bus.

The door shut in their faces and the bus farted its way noisily into the clogged road. Dan ran after it, banging on the window. "Stop! *Pasta!*"

"*Pasta?*" Amy said in bewilderment.

"I have a limited vocabulary!" Dan shouted. "*Linguini! Mangia! Buon giorno! Gucci!*"

A black limo screeched to a halt inches away, nearly hitting her.

"Gucci. I knew that would do it," Dan said.

The tinted window on the driver's side rolled down, and a man wearing sunglasses and a thick mustache calmly gestured for them to get in.

Amy opened the passenger door and climbed inside, yanking her brother in after her.

"Hey!" shouted another frantic passenger, pulling a wad of cash from his pocket and waving it at the driver through the window. "*Soldi, soldi!*"

Dan pulled his door shut, and three people fell on the car, banging and shouting. The driver turned forward and let his window roll up, nearly amputating the arm of the man with the money.

"Dude, thanks," Dan said to the driver. "Or *gracias* or whatever."

"Ve go to de udder airport?" the man replied in a deep accent that did not sound Italian.

"There's another airport?" Dan said.

"Small craft," the man replied.

"But—" Amy stammered. "We don't have any mon—"

Dan poked her in the ribs.

"I have to tell him the truth," Amy whispered.

Dan poked her again.

Amy glared at him. *"Will you please stop—?"*

It was only then that she saw the other person sitting in the backseat. An Asian man with a placid smile, dressed in a silk suit with white gloves and a bowler hat.

"Greetings, my elusive relatives," purred Alistair Oh.

CHAPTER 3

Alistair's father had always said that in every Oh there was an element of surprise.

Not that Alistair remembered him actually saying it, considering Alistair had been a child when he died. But it was an Oh family trait to mix truth with a touch of wit.

Alas, the Cahill children's hostile silence perplexed Alistair. He would have thought they'd have enjoyed this particular surprise.

Screeee . . . screeeee . . .

As Serge yanked the steering wheel left and right, forcing the car into spaces no normal human would dare to go, the children lurched from side to side. They seemed loathe to touch Alistair or even look at him, as if he were some distasteful substance, like boiled asparagus. As if he had not just snatched them from the jaws of chaos to deliver them back to their chosen path. He tried to smile reassuringly at them. He felt for them. They looked so small, so scared, so lonely.

He understood the feeling. More than they knew.

"Gyess what?" shouted Serge over the noise of furious honking. "*I* chave keeds, too—gerrl fourteen, boy elyeven! Yes! True. They leeve in Moscow!"

Alistair kept an eye on Dan, who was looking quite sick. The boy tried the door handle for what must have been the twentieth time in the last two minutes. Luckily, Alistair had made sure the safety locks had been activated. "Do not bother, please," he said. "You will only give yourself carpal tunnel problems later in life. And besides that, you are making me nervous for your safety."

"So you were behind all this, huh?" Dan said. "With the Kabras and Irina. And the bomb scare. You're working with them now."

Alistair's face twitched. He knew it would be difficult to earn their trust. Wild accusations were to be expected. He knew there would be resentment, and understandably so. Leaving them in a burning house on the day of the will reading had been an unfortunate necessity—but a personal and strategic mistake. One he regretted deeply. "Believe me, my dear nephew, I don't have the slightest idea—"

"Believe you?" Dan replied, spinning around to face him eye to eye. "Let's see. You abandoned us when Grace's house was collapsing around us. You planted a tracking device on Saladin—"

"Tracking device? *This?*" Alistair reached into his pocket and pulled out an electronic device the size of a lapel pin. "I believe you planted it on me. At the museum in Salzburg, while I was dozing."

"You d-d-deserved that, Uncle Alistair," Amy said uneasily, "after having hidden it in Saladin's collar in the f-f-first place."

"No again, darling girl," Alistair replied with a warm smile, hoping to calm the girl's nerves. "Someone else was keeping tabs on you. Not I. Remember, many others in the family are competing for the clues. I am on your side. I, as you know, believe in cooperation."

"Oh, that's hilarious," Dan shot back. "Tell it to Comedy Central."

Patience. Ever patience. Alistair folded his white-gloved hands over his lap. "Consider exactly who rescued you today," he said. "And who, in a very short time, managed not only to find you but to devise a method of escape. Consider also that as an added bonus, I am about to take you wherever it is you need to go. By private plane. All of this, and I ask only one thing in return — the location of where you are headed. Which, under the circumstances, is rather a necessity."

"You have your own p-plane?" Amy asked.

Alistair smiled modestly. "Well, not mine. But I still have business connections, favors I can call in during times of emergency. There are some financial advantages to being the inventor of microwavable burritos."

"Ve stock zem on ze plane!" Serge said. "Biff, cheecken, cheese . . . "

Good old Serge. Experience had taught them both the value of the Oh company motto: The way to a young person's heart is through microwavable meals.

Amy exhaled. "Okay, once we're on this plane—*if* we agree—what assurances do we have that—"

"*Amy!*" Dan blurted. "Uh, no way, Goldfinger. If we're going to do this, we're doing it ourselves."

Amy glared at him. "So I guess we're *swimming* to Japan? Drop us off at a mall, Uncle Alistair. I need flippers. The really big kind? With mad shark repellent?"

Dan groaned. "You said the J word, Amy! You *told* him!"

"What are our choices, Dan?" Amy said. "They have Nellie and Saladin and our s—"

Amy stopped short, and Alistair glanced at her encouragingly. The poor thing had been making such great progress with her shyness. "Your . . . ?" he said.

"S-s-suitcases," she replied.

Alistair nodded. *Japan.* Excellent. So that was where the next Clue would be. A fruitful turn of events. He leaned forward to his driver. "Can we handle Japan, Serge?"

The driver shrugged. "Vell, eez long treep. Ve must stop for refueling halfvay. In Moscow. I call ahead. Vhen ve stop, you can meet my keeds—Kolya and Tinatchka!"

"Serge, please," Alistair said. "This is not a social trip."

Serge let out a deep belly laugh. "Kolya and Tinatchka not socialists!"

Dan glared at his sister. *Swords*, she'd been about to say. *They have Nellie and Saladin and our swords.* At least she corked herself on that one. Giving away their destination to the slippery dude was one thing. Giving away their Clue was another. *Some* things had to stay secret. Even sisterus dorkus knew that.

He recognized the look in Amy's eyes right now. It was more than the usual disgust, more than her usual variations of *You dweeb* and *No, it's not time to eat.* This one said, *If you screw this up, I will kill you.*

Which was exactly how he was feeling.

Uncle Alistair reached into his pocket and pulled out two small electronic devices, which he held out to Dan and Amy with fake cheeriness, like a demented butler pretending to be Santa Claus. "These are state-of-the-art GPS devices. Attach them to your phones, as I have done to mine. I have not yet figured out how to one-twenty-eight-bit-encrypt the signal, but the lower default encryption should suffice. The point is, once we are in Japan, we cannot lose one another."

Serge was flashing an ID pass to a guard at a gate now. The limo entered a narrow road leading to a tiny airport. It glided past several small propeller planes and stopped next to a long, open hangar.

Serge quickly got out and held the passenger door open. Beaming, he gestured grandly toward the hangar. "Say hello to my darling Ludmila."

"Another keed?" Dan asked. "How many do you have?" He looked left and right. The place seemed empty except for a few small jets and some burly half-shaven crew members, none of whom looked like a Ludmila.

"Um . . . I don't see her," Amy said meekly.

But Dan was distracted by a flash of silver. A ridiculously sleek jet rolled into view. It had tinted windows, a profile like a knife, and an open cockpit that seemed to beckon, *Enter for the coolest ride of your life.*

"This," said Serge, as the jet rolled to a stop in front of them, "is Ludmila."

CHAPTER 4

The peculiar word COACH on Natalie's plane ticket had conjured up images of leather benches, uniformed coachmen, and fine horses.

Not tiny, hard seats and a pig.

It wasn't so much the babysitter's attitude. Which was horrid. Or the tattoos and piercings. Which some-day would cause the girl such embarrassment at her job—that is, should she ever find a real one. It wasn't even the girl's rudeness upon seeing Natalie and her brother. Granted, a warm hello and hugs were not warranted under the circumstances, but the stream of barnyard epithets was a bit . . . well, unseemly. To say the least.

Yet all of the above was to be expected from a person of Nellie's station. And Natalie and Ian could with-stand the crudeness. Some sacrifices were necessary in order to get the information they needed.

No, the worst part was the *sloppiness*. The candy wrappers and potato chip shards on the seats to either side of her, the backpack plopped on the floor between her feet instead of tucked under the seat in front. The nervous habit of shoveling fistfuls of snack mix into her mouth and chewing while speaking. Dreadful. *Sloppy habits make a sloppy mind*, according to the old Kabra family saying. Or maybe that was from *Bartlett's Familiar Quotations*. Natalie wasn't quite sure.

She winced as the loathsome babysitter spoke with a mouthful of food.

"Soffy, unca wassoosa, y'nah gongahwawee!" Nellie said, spitting bits of peanut and Chex from the corners of her mouth.

Natalie's brother, Ian, picked a fleck of Rice Krispie from his otherwise flawless jet-black hair. "Swallow, please, and repeat?"

Nellie gulped. "Sorry, I don't care what you say, you're not going to get away with this."

"Oh?" Ian looked over his shoulder, up and down the crowded jetliner. "Do I see anyone sympathizing with your plight? No? What do you say, Natalie—did we get away with it?"

"You can do this the easy way, you know, by answering one simple question . . . " Natalie pressed. They had asked Nellie a dozen times, and each answer had been sassier than the last. She would learn, though. If she knew what was good for her. And if not, well, the Kabras had other ways. "So. One last time—why are you going to Japan?"

Nellie yanked a magazine out of the seat pocket in front of her, sending a set of earphones and some used tissues flying toward Ian, who leaped with a barely concealed *yeep* of disgust. "Because I love sudoku," Nellie said. "You can get the best sudoku puzzles on a flight to Japan, duh. Don't you know *anything*?"

"Coffee, tea, complimentary snack packet, or anything else I can assist you with to make this your best flight ever?" a flight attendant piped up, walking slowly up the aisle.

"A Diet Coke and a restraining order, please?" Nellie said. "Because these two are *not* supposed to be in these seats, and they are harassing me."

Ian let out a hearty laugh. "Ha-ha! Oh, Cousin Nell, you always crack me up with your jokes and whatnot—doesn't she, uh, Amy?"

"Yes, Daniel," Natalie replied. "Just like back home. In . . . Homedale."

"Oh, that's convincing," Nellie said. "Is there a cop on board? Because if there's not, I want to make a citizen's arrest. Can you do that in Italy, or wherever we are?"

Smiling uneasily, the flight attendant placed a Diet Coke on Nellie's tray. As she stood back up, Natalie turned to the baffled woman and circled her finger by her ear in a subtle *cuckoo* gesture.

Outside the window, lightning flashed. The plane suddenly began to lurch. "Heh-heh, well, looks like we're experiencing just a bit of bumpiness here . . . " the pilot said over the PA.

The flight attendant began pushing her cart back up the aisle, calling out, "Please return your seats to the upright position."

Ian groaned. "I — I'm not feeling too well. . . ."

As he keeled forward, face turning green, it was Nellie's turn to look alarmed.

Natalie smiled. She and Ian had planned this. Certain signals for certain contingencies. Kabras were masters of tight planning. Ian's act meant one thing only, and Natalie knew just what to do.

Still, she couldn't help but feel pity for the girl. Underneath the raffishness there was a bit of spunk and spirit. In another circumstance, another time, she would make a good Kabra employee.

"Uh, you're not going to be sick, are you?" Nellie said. "Because I hate the sight of puke." She leaned forward to sift through all the detritus on the floor, looking for an air-sickness bag.

There.

While Nellie was turned away, Natalie reached into her pocket and extracted a small vial of dark liquid. With a deft motion, she lifted the vial to Nellie's soda. Two drops was all that was needed.

The plane jumped again, causing Natalie to flinch, and the entire contents of the vial spilled inside the Coke.

Oops.

The beeping of the phone woke Dan up from a deep sleep.

The first thing he noticed was Amy's hand, bone-white and clenching the armrest. "I don't know how you can sleep at a time like this . . ." she said through gritted teeth.

The little jet banked to the left, causing Amy to let out a scream. "Sweet!" Dan said. "Do that again, Serge!"

Serge laughed. "You like?"

"No!" Amy blurted.

Alistair was straining to hear the phone. "This is *who*?" he said, gesturing for everyone to be quiet. "Irina?"

Amy groaned.

"Yes, they did get away," Alistair said loudly. "They are with me, quite safe and sound . . . what? Did you say *Japan*?" Alistair let out a big laugh. "Oh, dear. You thought . . . you really believed that Dan and Amy didn't *let* the Kabra children take their tickets—that they didn't purposefully direct their babysitter to board the plane as a decoy . . . oh, my. Oh, that is rich . . . no no no, Irina. . . . What? You're breaking up. Perhaps you heard me wrong. Yes, OF COURSE THE CAHILLS ARE HEADED TO JAPAN. THAT IS EXACTLY RIGHT. Good-bye, dear."

"Um . . . what was that all about?" Dan said.

Alistair smiled. "I know Irina quite well. At this moment she is convinced you tricked the Kabras, not the other way around. And trust me, after what I just said, the last place in the world she suspects you to be going is Japan. . . . "

"Wait. You think you convinced her?" Dan said. "Uh, no offense, but that sounded pretty lame to me."

"I may be a failure in some things in my life, but I am a very quick study of people," Alistair replied. "I know exactly what works with Irina Spasky."

Amy turned her head toward Alistair, the color nearly drained from her face. He was a smart guy in many ways but a little old-fashioned. And he had overlooked something incredibly obvious.

"Don't . . . be too sure . . . " she said.

The pilot's voice, in Russian, called for clearance and quickly got it.

Banking to the right, the jet swooped low toward a small airport on the outskirts of Moscow. In the dry, parched landscape, the landing strip was a ghostly gray.

The lone passenger's fingers gripped the armrest as the wheels of the plane bumped against the ground. These landings were always rougher than she expected.

As the jet slowed, taxiing on the tarmac, she eyed the sleek silver Cessna being refueled. An impressive piece of machinery.

"Stop here," Irina said.

She could see the old man now, limping with his walking stick. He was dressed crisply and correctly, as always. The bowler and sunglasses gave that subtle touch of refinement. Irina liked a traditional man, not a slave to fashion. His clothes seemed a bit tight today, but during these stressful times, who hadn't put on weight?

A moment later, the little devils appeared, bundled in down coats and hats. Protected as always—first by Grace Cahill, now by the uncle. Why he had sold his soul to those two, she could never figure out. Someday he would learn.

They will betray you, Alistair, she thought, *unless you betray them first.*

She smiled. Thoughts of human weakness always picked up her spirits after a long trip. Back in her KGB days, betrayal came in so many colorful varieties—blackmail, white lies, red tape, yellow journalism.

Teams—paahh! she thought. Teams were of no use in discovering the 39 Clues. With a secret of this much power, jealousies were inevitable and no alliances would survive.

Irina would find the Clues by herself. Without lazy rich kids, over-the-hill taco tycoons, or dewy-eyed orphans. To them, the amateurs, this was a mysterious game. Not to Irina. The spoils, she knew, deserved to go to the one who had lost the most. To the lone wolf seeking justice. And vengeance.

Across the runway, the trio climbed into the jet. Irina leaned forward, glancing at her cell phone, which still showed the GPS coordinates and recipient of her last call: OH, ALISTAIR.

"'Oh, Alistair,' indeed," she said under her breath. "You are making this chase too easy for me . . . "

"Shto?" said her pilot.

"Follow them, Alexander."

He pulled the gearshift and the plane's engine hummed to life. Ahead of them, the Cessna was beginning to position for takeoff.

Now she would see if he was telling the truth about their ultimate destination.

She grinned. No one ever put anything over on Irina Spasky.

CHAPTER 5

Amy's brother was never comfortable in a new place until he committed an act of cluelessness. In Tokyo, it happened the morning after their arrival at the Thank You Very Much Hotel.

"Dan, you can't just *take* that—it's stealing," Amy said, watching him struggle to fit a hotel ashtray in his back pocket.

"They won't know it's missing!" Dan protested. "I need it for my collection."

Dan collected everything. If it fit in a house and wasn't chained to the floor, he had a collection for it.

"Your sister is correct," Uncle Alistair said sternly, stopping to lean on his walking stick on the way to the front door. He smelled of aftershave and powder. On the trip in from the airport, he had bought Amy and Dan a few changes of clothes and insisted they freshen up and have a long sleep.

Amy had not slept for a nanosecond. For one thing, she was too nervous. For another, Dan kept muttering *"Mrrp"* in his sleep. He was really missing Saladin.

But that hadn't curbed his obsession for collecting. Amy held out her palm. Reluctantly, Dan put the ashtray in it. "Okay, but can you get me a Thank You Very Much Hotel matchbook, then?" he asked.

Amy returned the ashtray to a table in the lobby, with Dan skulking behind. They still couldn't pronounce the hotel's real name. Instead, they nicknamed it after the only phrase any of the staff ever said to them. Picking up a matchbook from the front desk, Amy smiled at the desk clerk. "Thank you very much!" the clerk said.

As they walked back toward the door, Dan eyed Alistair, who was looking away from them. "Let's escape," Dan murmured. "We have to find our peeps. Nellie and Saladin."

"Are you crazy?" Amy whispered back. "Uncle Alistair paid for this hotel stay. He knows Japanese, and he's going to help us around town."

"You like him!" Dan said in horror. "He's turned your mind!"

Amy whirled on him. "I don't like him *or* trust him. But without him we're stuck, Dan. So we have to *pretend,* at least until Nellie finds us."

"Or we find her!" Dan grumbled as he and Amy headed toward Alistair at the front entrance. Together they stepped out into a crisp, sunny day. To their left, people in manga-hero costumes greeted shoppers in front of a gleaming high-rise shopping center. The scent of some strange blossom wafted from a park, which was across a busy street filled with car and bike traffic. Tokyo reminded Amy of New York City, without all the people yelling at each other.

Dan's eyes were cast upward, gawking at a steel structure that rose above the park. "Cool, someone brought over the Eiffel Tower and painted it red and white!"

Alistair smiled. "The Tokyo Tower is taller than its Parisian counterpart, but also lighter, due to advances in steel construction — advances that were developed, may I add, by an Ekat engineer. My illustrious family. And you see that tall apartment tower with curved sides? It suggests a Japanese flower found in great abundance in Shiba Park. The brainchild of a Janus architect — "

"Wait, that park has flowers made of steel?" Dan said.

"I know someone with a brain made of tin," Amy replied, then turned back to Alistair. "How do you know so much about your family?"

"Someday I will show you my collection," Alistair said. "But let's get to the task at hand. It is a ten-minute cab ride to the Metropolitan Library."

"Library. Woo-hoo. Can't wait," Dan said, absently fingering his matchbook. "Hey, I know. You guys go. I'll pick up some snapper sushi and take a cab to the airport. I'll meet you later."

"What makes you think Saladin is at the airport?" Alistair asked, walking toward the street.

"I figure two things could have happened," Dan said. "One—the Kabras brainwashed Nellie and are leading her around town trying to find us. Or Two—Nellie managed to subdue them with superior ninja training techniques she didn't realize she had picked up by mental telepathy from me. Actually, I'm betting on One. Either way, Saladin would . . . " Dan's face darkened. "I—I can't stop thinking of him, still on that conveyor belt, all alone, going round and round . . . "

"I know you love your pet," Alistair said. "But you must think of your own safety first. The Kabras will expect you to come to Japan. They may also expect you to go to the airport in search of your beloved feline and babysitter—"

"Au pair," Dan corrected him.

"You simply cannot risk walking into a trap," Alistair continued.

It made Amy sick not to know where Nellie and Saladin were, too. She'd been trying to contact Nellie on her cell phone since they arrived. She hated telling Dan not to go after them. But Alistair's advice made sense. "Knowing Natalie and Ian," Amy said, following Alistair toward a taxi stand, "they'll find us."

"But—" Dan protested.

"We have to move forward," Amy said. "Nellie will land on her feet."

Dan sighed. "Saladin, too, I guess. I mean, being a cat and all . . . "

As they threaded their way through the plaza, Dan kept lighting matches and blowing them out. "Will you stop it?" Amy said.

"Why?" Dan said, lighting another match. "It's fun. It keeps my mind off the fact that here we are ignoring the only two people we really like, plus we're in the land of ninjas and Mothra and really cool martial arts, and we're going to spend another day in a library."

As he approached a waiting taxicab, Alistair said something to the driver in rapid, fluent-sounding Japanese and signaled Amy and Dan to climb in.

They sped through the traffic, passing rows of modern steel buildings and an occasional ornate ancient pagoda surrounded with gardens. "Why can't we stay in one of those cottages?" Dan asked.

"They are ancient temples," Alistair replied. "You will see more of them as we approach our destination. The military dictator — the shogun — ordered all temples moved here. At the time, the Roppongi area was a remote outpost of the capital, which was then called Edo. Part of the area was a hunting ground for the shogunate."

"Fascinating," Amy said. She loved learning about the origins of cities.

Dan nodded, staring dully out the window. "I think I just saw a celebrity."

Alistair's cell phone rang. "Hello . . . ? Yes . . . ah, bravo, Serge. She *what*? Well, imagine that—ha! Very good. And thank you so much. *Da. Do svidanya!*"

He put the phone away and turned to Dan and Amy. "Serge is safely in Siberia with his two children. Irina completely fell for the disguise. She thought they were we. When she realized she'd been had, she began cursing with words that embarrassed even Serge."

"Yes!" Dan whooped, slapping high fives to his sister and uncle.

"I have you to thank, Amy," Alistair said, beaming. "How stupid of me not to realize Irina could have tracked us with the cell phone GPS."

"I thought of it, like, right away," Dan said modestly. "I'm just more shy."

Amy rolled her eyes. "And I'm the queen of England."

"You *do* look wrinkly and boring," Dan said.

He darted away before Amy could whack him.

Soon the cab pulled up to a massive, modern, boxlike building at the edge of a lush park.

"Arisugawanomiya!" the cabdriver announced.

Dan looked panic-stricken. "What did I do now?"

"It is the name of the park, and that building is the Central Branch of the Tokyo Metropolitan Library," Alistair explained, as he paid the driver and climbed out. "We have only limited time before Irina catches on. Because we've detached our GPS devices, it is essential that we stay close together. And set your phones to 'vibrate' while in the library."

"How can I stand the excitement?" Dan droned.

The moment they entered the building, a trim librarian was at Alistair's side, bowing and speaking with him in rapid Japanese. She smiled at Dan and Amy and gestured for them to follow her.

"You know her?" Dan whispered as they climbed a grand marble staircase. "Like from back in your shogun-hunting days?"

"No, she is just being courteous," Alistair replied, his limp barely noticeable as he walked. "It is respect for my age. Although perhaps Ms. Nakamura remembers my television appearances ten years ago. My company's Terribly Tasty Teriyaki microwavable burritos were quite the rage."

They entered a small private room lined with bookcases. On one wall a couple of small windows overlooked the street. In the center was a bank of computers. "Please do not hesitate to come to me with any questions," Ms. Nakamura said in lightly accented English, exchanging bows with Alistair and shutting the door behind her.

"I told her we were conducting research for a new interactive website on possible burrito fillings," Alistair said, resting both hands on his walking stick as he leaned toward Amy and Dan. "But my question to you is, why are we *really* here?"

Amy's eyes darted over to Dan. Alistair had asked this question before, and they had evaded him each time. He knew they were up to something.

The problem was the swords. Alistair didn't know about them. He hadn't seen the secret engraving on one of the blades. He had no idea that the second Clue had been tungsten.

He's even more confused than we are, Amy thought. Iron solute and tungsten weren't exactly obvious interlocking puzzle pieces. The first was an ingredient in ink, the second was the material that burns in incandescent lightbulbs. How could they fit together? Amy and Dan needed to know so much more — but one thing was pretty clear. Somehow the swords were the key to the next Clue. Maybe Alistair *could* help them find out, Dan thought. But the risks were great. Alistair just might take the info and run; he'd done it before. *Trust no one* — that had been Amy and Dan's motto. Whenever they'd forgotten it, they'd regretted it.

And they desperately needed to limit regrets.

"It was . . . a code," Dan said, improvising a white lie. "In the music. Mozart's music. The code said, um, 'Go to Japan.' In the key of C? That's all we know."

Alistair shrugged, sitting at a laptop. "Not much to go on, but that hasn't stopped us before. Let's each work awhile and then compare notes, shall we?"

Amy and Dan made sure to sit opposite him, so their monitors were not visible to Alistair. Amy typed into a search bar:

japan tungsten sword
87,722 hits.

"This is going to be a long day," murmured Amy.

Dan typed:

ninja warrior images
1,694,117 hits.

He smiled. Maybe it wouldn't be so bad after all.

> Body painting and the tatoo was the
> belonging to slaves and prisoner of
> Ancint Japan. some of design has been
> historical replication by ours tattoo
> artists all who is graduate of colleges in
> history dilpoma.

Dan scrolled down. The images were clearer than the English translation. Some of these designs were amazing, covering a person's whole back. There were dozens — dragons, historical scenes, countrysides, ornate scrollwork . . .

He stopped. Something in one of the images looked familiar.

Scooting back up the page, he found it and clicked through. Slowly, a magnified version filled the screen.

"Dan, *what* do you think you're doing?" Amy asked, looking over his shoulder.

"Is this cool or what?" Dan said.

Amy gestured to her laptop screen, which showed a map of Japan. "We're supposed to be locating our clue!"

"Uh, excuse me, Dora the Explorer, look closely—these characters? They are the same ones we saw on the sword!"

Oops.

Dan's hands immediately shot up to his mouth. He hadn't meant to say the S word.

Amy's eyes went all buggy. *Dan, you moron!* they said silently.

Dan and Amy glanced at Alistair, who had been intently writing down something he was seeing on his screen. Slowly he looked up. He seemed pale, almost sick.

"Uncle Alistair . . . ?" Dan said. "Are you okay?"

Alistair did not answer for a few seconds. He took off his glasses and wiped them with a pocket handkerchief. "Fine. Staring at the screen for long periods of time . . . it gets harder to do when you're old. Forgive me. Have you, er, found anything?"

"Yes," said Dan.

"No," said Amy.

"Yes and no," clarified Dan. "Have you?"

Alistair nodded absently. "Come. Look."

Amy and Dan scooted around to see Alistair's screen. He was minimizing a webmail site to reveal a web page that showed a painting of a fierce-looking

Japanese warrior holding a severed head.

"Eww . . ." Amy murmured.

"Dude, it's only pixels," Dan said. "But . . . eww."

"The, um, Bald Rat," Alistair continued, his voice still faraway and distracted. "Also known as Toyotomi Hideyoshi."

"Hidewhoshi?" Dan replied.

"He—he was the greatest warrior in the history of Japan," Alistair went on, "but most records show him as rather hideous-looking. Lived in the fifteen hundreds. He began as a peasant and rose to unbelievable power, conquering the various tribes and factions and uniting the country as a major power for the first time." Alistair paused, lowering his voice. "He was also one of your Cahill ancestors—"

"I *thought* I saw the resemblance to Amy," Dan said.

"—A Tomas, as a matter of fact. Descended from Thomas Cahill. Thomas traveled to the Far East in the sixteenth century—some say for the purposes of trade, others say to hide in shame after failing to find his wayward sister. At any rate, he settled there and his family became the Tomas branch, famous for their brutishness and warrior ways."

Dan looked closer. "The Holt family—they're Tomases. They look like tree trunks with dinosaur brains. This guy looks like a weasel."

"It makes sense Hideyoshi would be a Tomas," Amy said. "The strength. The gross way he's holding that head."

"Evolution is odd. It does not favor the Tomas." Alistair's grim expression loosened a bit, edging into a semismile. "Of course, I am showing my bias as an Ekat. Anyway, I strongly believe our search should begin with Hideyoshi. The man had a lot of secrets. Some say the secrets undid him."

"Secrets is our middle name, dude," Dan said.

Alistair leveled his gaze at Dan and then Amy. The color was returning to his face now. "I was going to keep this information to myself. After what happened in Salzburg, I wasn't sure I could trust you two. In fact, today I was tempted to conduct this entire search for the Hideyoshi link without your knowledge."

"Well, that makes two of us," Dan blurted out.

"Three," Amy corrected. With a quick, tentative glance toward Dan, she added, "We didn't think we could trust *you,* Uncle Alistair."

Alistair nodded. "I have devoted myself to earning your confidence again. Trust is a fragile thing — difficult to build, easy to break. It cannot be bargained for. Only if it is freely given can it be expected in return." He looked from Amy to Dan. "To break the chain of mistrust, someone has to go first. I am happy to make the move. You deserve no less."

Solemnly, he turned back to his screen. "Hideyoshi was a bit of a paranoid who liked to hoard things," Alistair continued, scrolling down the screen into the biographical text. "For example, the Great Sword Hunt of 1588, when he forced all the farmers and peasants to give over their swords. He claimed he wanted to melt them down for a large statue of Buddha. But that was a lie."

"And the truth was . . . ?" Amy said.

Alistair shrugged. "One of the great mysteries. He also took measures to prevent farmers and peasants from rising to the warrior class. He seemed to be afraid of this."

"But *he* rose from the poor," Amy said.

"You must think like a warrior, sister-san," Dan said. "He was afraid *because* he rose from the poor. He thought somebody else might, too — and whup his ninja butt."

Alistair nodded. "Perhaps he suspected more Tomas offspring — or worse, Ekaterina — lived in the provinces. The Ekat and Tomas branches were at war even then. Was he trying to hide swords from the Ekats to prevent them from rising against him? We don't know. If only we knew *where* he hid the swords. The *where* might lead to the *why*." With a shrug, Alistair turned to face them. "Okay, I've told you all I know."

Dan glanced at his sister. The ball was in their court now.

He's shown us his own secrets, her eyes were saying. *We owe him.*

He was looking at his webmail, Dan thought in return. *He didn't show us THAT.*

That's different, she argued. *We need him.*

Besides his cash and his knowledge of Japanese, what good is he?

Besides your nicely shaped left earlobe, what good are you?

Dan glowered at her. *You're the oldest, YOU mention it.*

Amy turned to Alistair. "We think . . . we found some of the swords," she said. "In Venice."

"Hideyoshi's swords — in *Italy*?" Alistair looked flabbergasted.

With a sigh, Dan mumbled, "They were in the house of some Italian dude, Fidelio Racco."

"Racco . . . " Alistair said. "A Janus. Yet the clue points to a Tomas stronghold. Curious. Here in Japan, there are rumored to be secret Hideyoshi hiding places, but they are allegedly guarded by the descendants of Hideyoshi — many of them *yakuza*."

Dan smiled. *Now* he was talking. "Whoa — awesome!" Dan exclaimed. "I battled them at Level Four in . . . um, *Ninja Gaiden,* I think? Those guys are mad gangsta! They'll cut off your arms and feed them to you for lunch."

"Can't wait to meet them," Amy said.

"We tried to bring the swords here," Dan barreled on. "They're in my luggage. One of them had some markings. We figured the markings were important—maybe they give information about the next clue."

Alistair's eyes widened. "Is there any way we can retrieve these swords?"

"Well, maybe we don't have to." Dan nodded to his screen. "The same markings are on this tattoo."

Dan had never seen Alistair move so fast. He leaned over Dan's shoulders and squinted at the image. "Are you *sure* this was printed on the sword?"

"Yup," Dan said. "Well, not exactly. There were some other characters, too. They're missing here."

Amy shook her head. "How can you be sure? You don't know a word of Japanese."

"Uh, yeah," Dan said. "And I don't read a note of music. But let's see, who was the one who *memorized a whole Mozart song and found our last clue*? Wait, wait, let me try to remember. Oh. I know—me!"

"Dan, are you *sure* there were characters missing?" Alistair said. "Because the message, as is, is fairly innocuous—an incantation to luck, honor, triumph, and such."

"Definitely. At the beginning of each line, there was some weird-looking letter. Like from another language. You know, Sanscript maybe."

"It's Sanskr*it*, tattoo-brain," Amy said, sitting at her laptop. "Guess you don't remember *everything* perfectly."

She turned to her uncle, who was furiously tapping on his keyboard. "What do you know about these *yakuza* people, Uncle Alistair?"

She thought she could feel him shudder. "They are very nasty and very deadly," he said softly. "Trust me, we do not want to cross their paths."

"You know some of them personally?" Dan said.

"They know me and despise me," Alistair said. "I am an Ekat. The Tomas and the Ekats have been bitter enemies for centuries. The *yakuza* have long been suspected to possess a map to a secret underground crypt. And if I am to understand this recent message, we may have found a copy."

He hit the PRINT button. From the library's printer, a map slowly made its way into the paper tray, an ancient image showing a complicated ribbon of tunnels.

"Cool!" Dan exclaimed.

"You *knew* about this all along?" Amy asked.

Alistair shook his head. Once again, his face became pale and drawn. "I have long been searching for certain . . . stolen Ekat documents not related to this. One of my colleagues has managed to find a hidden cache. I received a message from him on webmail while we were in Salzburg, with several attachments—including this map."

He showed them the printout, which had the heading OF UNKNOWN SIGNIFICANCE.

"Wait—Ekat documents? *Colleagues?* What else are you keeping from us? How can you—?"

Amy's words stopped in her throat. The cursor on Dan's monitor was moving from the middle of the screen up to the left corner.

"Dan?" Amy said. "Stop that, okay?"

"Stop what?" Dan replied.

"We know libraries bore you, but can't you take *anything* seriously?" Amy replied. "You're playing a trick, right? You have something in your pocket and it's sending a signal to the computer. Otherwise, *why would the cursor be moving?*"

Now the cursor was on the BACK button, clicking rapidly through every page Dan had visited—tattoos, information about Hideyoshi and the Sword Hunt, the Facebook pages of three sixth-grade girls—

"Hey!" Dan shouted.

"It's a keylogger," Alistair said, swiftly picking up the laptop. "Someone has hacked into the computer remotely and is spying on everything you've looked at today."

With a solid yank, he pulled the electric plug from the back, and the screen went dead. A steady beeping noise began, and an LCD panel by the light switch flashed red Japanese characters that looked suspiciously like some form of EMERGENCY.

"How did they do it?" Amy asked.

Dan took the laptop, examining the PC card. "It's an 802.11g wireless," he said. "So they have to be pretty close. I don't know, maybe like thirty yards—or fifty if they have a booster or something?"

Alistair headed for the window. "Which means either they're in the building or in one of those cars outside."

One of those *hundreds* of cars, he could have said — if you considered the cars at the curb, in the nearby parking lot, and bumper-to-bumper on the road.

Tap-tap-tap-tap!

The rapping on the door made them all jump. "Is everything all right in there?" a tiny, timid voice called in.

It sounded like Ms. Nakamura, but there was something about her tone . . .

Alistair went to the door. "She may know how to run a trace."

"No!" Amy blurted out.

"Ms. Nakamura," Alistair said, yanking the doorknob, "your library has been compromised —"

The door flew open — and Alistair was staring into the massive chest of a gray XXXL T-shirt.

"No kidding, Sherwood," said Eisenhower Holt, with a grin so wide it nearly touched the edges of his stiff military brush cut. "Now, fall in line, all of you — and *march!*"

CHAPTER 6

Dzzzzz . . .

Amy's phone was vibrating.

She glanced around the van. In the passenger seat, Eisenhower Holt was arguing with his wife, Mary-Todd, who was driving. In the next row, eleven-year-olds Madison and Reagan Holt were having a contest to see who could fling boogers into the hair of their older brother, Hamilton. Their pit bull, Arnold, barked greedily, snatching the small projectiles in mid flight with his massive jaws.

"Stop it, he'll kill me!" Ham cried.

"That's the point," Madison replied, clapping her hands.

"Sherwood is the *forest*, dear," Mary-Todd was insisting to her husband. "The detective was Sher*lock*."

"We'll look it up!" Eisenhower declared. "May I remind you, Mary-Todd, at West Point my IQ was measured at nearly a perfect one hundred. Well, okay, eighty-nine—but I hadn't even practiced!"

"One hundred is considered *normal*, sugar maple," Mary-Todd replied.

"Normal is the enemy of creativity," Eisenhower crowed. "A Holt is *never* normal—as evidenced by our ingenious capture of the Cahills!"

Dzzzzz . . .

Amy moved her hand into her left pants pocket and pulled out her phone, making sure to keep it out of sight. On the right, she was jammed up against Alistair, who was seething with rage. He in turn was jammed up against Dan—who seemed oblivious, reading a handful of tourist pamphlets the Holts had left on the van floor.

Quickly she glanced at the call screen:

GOMEZ, NELLIE

She stifled a scream and stared sharply at Alistair and Dan, flashing the screen at them at waist level.

Nellie was alive!

"YESSSS—WOO-HOO!" Dan blurted.

"The Cahill boy agrees with me!" Eisenhower said with a grin, turning around toward the back of the van. "Smart boy. You're going places. Like, with *us*—as a captive! Har-har!"

The entire Holt family cracked up, except for Arnold, who seemed confused by the sudden absence of flying minitreats.

"Too bad you weren't smart enough to detect us following you every step of the way," Eisenhower continued, "with our patented Holt hackment technology. First we hacked into the tracking device on your cat—until we found that your cat was your uncle!"

Madison and Reagan looked at him in total bewilderment.

"Then we tailed him to the airport, where I ordered that we attempt the greatest technicological feat of all," Eisenhower went on, "breaking into the airline ticketing mainframe!"

"But then I reminded him that all he needed to do was follow your limo," Mary-Todd spoke up.

Madison chimed in: "Once we were at the other airport? And we saw you get into the jet? We just asked this really hot flight guy, Fabio? Where you were going?" She grinned. "And he told us."

"Rawf," said Arnold.

"Thusly," Eisenhower said, "we were able to commandeer our own flight to Japan, where we beat you to the airport and waited until you arrived, following your every move until our ultimate coup—keyloggering your very laptop to filch all your information! And now that I have you three, I can realize my life's goal. Not just reaching the thirty-nine clues first. But placing the Holt name where it belongs—at the very crest of the Tomas family . . . crest. No longer will history look upon the Holts as dolts. No longer will we be the black sheep, the stain on the family underpants, the smelly footnote to the Tomas legend. And you will help us achieve our destiny by leading us to the very thing your research revealed—the next clue, which is in the tunnels of Tokyo!"

"You figured that out all by yourself?" Amy asked, barely containing the relief she felt at knowing her au pair was okay.

"About fifty-three percent of it," said Eisenhower.

"More like forty-seven," Mary-Todd said.

"I knew that sounded wrong," Eisenhower said.

"Uh, Dad? *I* was the one who did all that tech stuff," Reagan whined.

"Dad *what*?" Eisenhower commanded.

"Dad, sir," Reagan said.

"Your argument is as inane as your conversation," Alistair spoke up, his voice a barely controlled rasp. "You got nothing from hacking the system. You stole my map, you windbag."

"Uncle Alistair?" Amy said. She had never seen him like this.

"Is someone meowing back there?" Eisenhower said. "Do I hear an E-*kat*?"

"*Rawf?*" said Arnold, suddenly drooling.

Alistair laughed defiantly. "What makes you miscreants think you can actually read that map correctly? It's written in Japanese."

"Ha! No grass grows over the head of a Holt!" Eisenhower thundered. "I overheard you through the library door, talking about an ancient underground crypt. So we will start at . . . the underground crypt district. *Harch!*"

The van lurched to the left.

Dan looked up from a map of the Tokyo subway system. His face was all lit up, the way it was whenever he'd broken a code or discovered a cheat in *World of Warcraft*. "Crypt? I think we're better off checking out the subway system."

The van lurched to the right.

"I have to pee," Madison announced.

The van skidded to a stop on the shoulder of the road. "Will someone make a decision?" Mary-Todd said.

As the Holts ramped up their various arguments, Alistair whispered to Dan, "Subway system, my boy? Do tell."

"First, I memorized your map," Dan began with a bit too much enthusiasm.

"Ssshhh!" Amy hissed.

"The secret tunnels and the subway," Dan barreled on. "They match — almost exactly! I'm figuring maybe the subway was built into the already existing tunnels!"

The Holts shut up at once.

"*Dan —*" Amy warned. "You're telling this to *them*!"

Dan looked up, bewildered. "I was telling Uncle Alistair."

"But we-ee-ee heard you," Reagan sang in a taunt, and stuck out her tongue. "Besides, if you hadn't told us, you'd be dead meat."

"*Rawf*," said Arnold, baring his saliva-glistened incisors.

Dan's face turned white. He cast a guilty look at Amy and at Alistair, whose face had become suddenly cloudy. "Um, well . . . the thing is? It's not really a match. So I was wrong. 'Cause, um, there's this big difference. In the center of the old map, there's an intersection with a large room. In the subway map, the tracks are parallel. So . . . see? It must be the wrong place. . . . "

"Where two maps diverge is precisely where the secret might be!" Eisenhower crowed.

"Brilliant as always!" Mary-Todd said.

Amy groaned. The stupider Dan became, the smarter it made Eisenhower Holt.

"Sweet," said Hamilton with a sneer.

Suddenly, Eisenhower spun on them with narrowed eyes. "Now, you're not trying to trap us, are you? We're not as dumb as we look. Or . . . whatever."

"Well . . . " Dan looked helplessly from Amy to Alistair. "There are subway stops on either side. I'm fig-uring the one at the northern end, Yotsuya, is closer."

"We'll take the one at the southern end," Eisenhower commanded.

The van lurched into the road again.

"Now I really have to pee," said Madison.

They waited silently until the train left Nagatacho station. They were the only ones on the subway platform now. The train schedule, which Alistair had picked up from the attendant, said that the next train arrived at 5:40. He checked his watch.

Then he looked down at the tracks — the *dark*, *narrow* tracks that led into a pitch-black tunnel on either side.

"It's five-seventeen," he said, his voice shaking. "We have exactly twenty-three minutes."

Eisenhower stepped to the edge of the platform. "Fall in, troops!" he said.

"I want to go first!" Madison said.

"She kept us waiting when she was in the bathroom," Reagan complained. "Can *I* go? Please?"

"It's almost Mom's birthday," Hamilton said.

"Rawf," said Arnold, diving over the edge to chase a soot-blackened rat that skittered across the tracks.

"Every Holt for himself!" Eisenhower cried, pulling green gardener's gloves from his pocket, snapping them on, and lowering himself over the edge. "Be sure not to touch the fourth rail!"

"Third, hug-muffin," Mary-Todd said.

As Madison and Reagan followed, Alistair took Dan's and Amy's arms and stepped slowly backward. He was trying to escape. But Mary-Todd and Hamilton stood in his path, arms folded. "Uh-uh-uh!" Hamilton tutted.

"Nice try, Uncle," Dan whispered.

It was 5:19. Twenty-one minutes left.

With a sigh, Dan climbed onto the track, followed by Amy, Alistair, and the remaining Holts. A stream, inky black, ran between the rails. A gum wrapper floated by. Ahead of them, the tunnel plunged into blackness. Dan felt woozy. He and Amy hadn't had much luck in underground places. Images began floating in his brain. *Running . . . running . . . from Jonah Wizard in a subterranean museum in Venice . . . from the Kabras in the Catacombs under Paris . . . from a train . . . from a memory . . .* He could still feel Amy's hand yanking him away from the approaching subway car in Paris, his backpack disappearing underneath the tons of speeding steel, the scream ripping from his throat. To anyone else, the faded snapshot he'd kept in that pack—the smiling couple—would have seemed blurry and uninteresting. But to Dan, it was as important as life. He had looked at it every day, memorized every last pixel. It was the only memento, the only remaining image of the parents he barely remembered. And now it was gone, a continent away.

"Hup-two-three-four . . . " Eisenhower called out.

Amy pulled Dan forward, shaking the memory from his brain. *Splash-splash-splash-thwuck,* went his footsteps. *"Thwuck?"* he squeaked.

"Don't ask," said Amy. Even in the near-blackness, Dan could tell her face was bone-white.

They trudged onward, keeping to the middle of the track to avoid the third rail, until the dimming light of the station behind them faded to nothing. "RePORT on proGRESS!" Eisenhower called out.

Dan's hands shook as he shone his pocket flashlight on the subway map. Ahead of them, the light of the next station was barely visible. They had passed the halfway point. "According to this," Dan said, "we should be about there now. The intersection would have been to our left."

"At ease!" Eisenhower said. "Fall in to examine hidden methods of egress!"

Amy reached out to her left, feeling along the grime-covered surface. "Nothing there but a wall."

"Keep trying," Eisenhower said.

Dan frantically pushed and punched, but the wall was solid. Thick cement. He checked his watch, which was already beginning to lose its glow-in-the-dark properties.

5:30.

"Th-this was a dumb idea," he said, his voice echoing dully in the tunnel. "Look, we have ten minutes. We left the station eleven minutes ago. We have enough time to get back before—"

"Abort mission!" Eisenhower barked. "Dress left! And . . . *hut-two-three-four*!"

Dan began to run, nearly tripping over his sister.

"Ow!" Amy cried out. *"Dan!"*

"Sorry!" Dan said. "See you at the platform—"

"Dan, my foot is stuck!"

Dan whirled around and shone his flashlight on Amy's crouching silhouette. She was grimacing, her left foot jammed under one of the rails.

"I'll rescue her!" Hamilton shouted.

"No, me!" Reagan shrieked. "I never get to rescue first!"

"Stand clear!" Eisenhower boomed.

"Rawf," Arnold barked.

Dan elbowed his way into the crowd, trying to reach his sister, who was screaming at the top of her lungs, *"You're only making it worse!"*

Dan's hair began to rise in swirls lightly from the back of his head. A low but steady wind was gusting through the tunnel from the south. Dan could see Amy's face looking up to him, eyes wide. "Dan? How accurate are those train tables?"

"I don't know!" Dan replied.

"When a train is entering a t-tunnel, don't you f-feel the air being pushed — ?"

Ho-o-o-o-o-o-o-onk!

Dan spun toward the sound. Two distant headlights, like reptilian eyes piercing the darkness, were headed their way—and growing fast.

"Holts—*bolt*!" Eisenhower commanded.

As one, the Holt family turned away from the approaching train and broke for the next station at a dead run.

"Don't leave us!" Amy shouted.

Dan pulled and pulled. Amy's foot was jammed. Tight.

"OWWWW!"

"I'll . . . get . . . it," Dan said through gritted teeth. He knelt in the icy trickle of water running between the rails, now choppy with the vibrations.

"Run, Dan!"

"Wait . . . I know . . . "

The laces. Dan dug his fingers into her shoelaces and yanked hard.

They were knotted. Wet and stuck. Her foot seemed glued to the shoe. If he could just slip it out, use the wetness to slide . . .

The screech of the brakes filled the tunnel. The wind whipped around him like a gale, throwing dust and debris into his eyes. His vision flashed white. His body was telling him to go. Now.

"JUST RUN!"

"Stop it, Amy, I can't leave you —"

She had saved him. He could save her. He had to do it.

Pull!

The wind was violent. The noise pressed into his ears like a solid thing. He pulled again, wiggled, jerked, pounded.

She was resisting now, pushing him away—trying to save him. Her breath felt cold on his neck, the veins in her throat bulging out.

He realized she was shrieking, but he couldn't hear a word.

HO-O-O-O-O-O-O-O-ONK!

Dan's body froze solid as he turned into the glare of the oncoming headlights.

CHAPTER 7

"AHHHHHH!"

Amy didn't feel much at all. The wind. The metallic shriek of the brakes, the horn blocking out all sound.

She must have closed her eyes, because she didn't see anything, either.

She felt.

Her body wrenched upward and backward. She was flying.

And then her shoulder hit solid, cold cement.

When she opened her eyes, all was dark and silent.

"I g-g-guess . . . I'm dead?" she heard her own voice call out, strangely high-pitched and thin.

For a long time, she heard nothing else. And then:

"Hi, Dead. I'm Dan."

The *ssshhhhick* of a lit match sounded, and a tremulous light outlined two faces.

Amy sat up. Her left ankle ached, and her shoe was missing. "Uncle Alistair? Dan?"

Dan's hair was standing on end, his face shadowed with black dust and his eyes the size of softballs. "He did it. Uncle Alistair. He saved our lives. Reached out. From the wall. How—?" Dan tottered toward her, his body bent over as he gawked at Amy's foot. "It's still there. He didn't amputate it when he —"

With that, Dan's knees buckled and he crumpled to the floor.

"Dan!" Amy shouted. As she reached out to grab his arm, her ankle screamed with pain.

"It's all right," Dan said, sitting up. "I'm all right. Don't call nine-one-one. Did my hair turn white? Like in movies, like when people get really, really scared?"

"You're both safe now," Alistair said, moving his match around to outline the contours of a large room. "Dan, your hair is not white—and you were right about the hiding place. It is more or less where you thought it would be. There was a small graffito, an ancient-looking symbol on what looked like an electrical plate. Once I pressed it, the door swung open. I merely brought you both in with me."

Amy lunged forward on her good foot, keeping the other one in the air, and flung her arms around him. "Thank you," she said.

She felt him flinch. For a horrible moment she felt as if she'd done something terribly wrong. She could tell he was not the hugging type. Then, awkwardly, Alistair wrapped his arms around her. "I . . . owed you one," he said softly.

"Or two," Dan said.

Alistair nodded. "I suppose my record is not very good in life-threatening situations."

"Well, you've made up for it now," Amy said, burying her head in the shoulder of Alistair's silk suit jacket, which still smelled of aftershave.

Gently, Alistair pulled himself away, glancing downward with concern. "How does your foot feel?"

"Like it was jammed under a rail and then pulled out of its shoe," Amy said with a wince. "I can move it, but I think I sprained my ankle."

"Bet you can't tap-dance," Dan said, still sounding a little shell-shocked.

Amy smiled at her brother, never *ever* having imagined she would enjoy hearing his stupid humor. She felt a rush of warmth for him.

"Oh, no, I see that look—*no* hugs!" Dan said, backing away.

Numbly, he flicked on his flashlight and swept it slowly around the room, until the beam landed on a pile of old relics lying haphazardly on the floor and covered with thick, gray-black dust—clothing, strange tarnished metal things, a metal box, a globe, a hefty cylinder. As they all moved closer, Alistair remarked, "Well, the *yakuza* may control some kind of underground network, but it doesn't look like they've been here in a few centuries."

"Hey," Dan piped up. "What does Jar Jar Binks say when he meets a member of the Japanese Mafia?"

Amy groaned. "You are recovering too quickly."

"I'm game. Wait . . . " Alistair paused for a moment and smiled. "'You, sah? *Yakuza*?'"

Dan's grin disappeared. "How did you know that? I just made it up out of my own head."

"Puns are a sign of intelligence, deeply buried," Alistair replied, putting on his white gloves. He leaned into the pile of stuff and gingerly lifted a small, brittle garment. "Hard to tell how old this is under so many decades of metal dust."

"Hey, check it out!" Dan said. He was unrolling a scroll that he'd pulled from behind a chest of drawers.

"Careful!" Amy said.

The scroll was open now, blackened around the edges but legible — three lines of stylized Japanese characters. "What's it say?" Dan asked.

Alistair looked closely. "It's a haiku, I think. Wait, let me get the meter right. . . . 'To find the new home/ Of Hideyoshi's treasure/Use geometry.'"

"Treasure?" Amy said. "Does that include the swords?"

"We're rich!" Dan shouted. "Woo-hoo — I knew it! Okay, geometry. I'll get this one. Hang on, give me a minute. . . . "

"It could be anything . . . " Amy said, gazing around the room.

"We're in a big room," Dan declared. "So . . . the volume of a parallelepiped, maybe?"

"Beg pardon?" Alistair said.

"A three-dimensional parallelogram, like this chamber," Dan explained.

"How would *that* solve the problem?" Amy asked. "It's like trying to find a hypotenuse in a haystack."

"Is that a joke?" Dan said. "Because if it is, you should give me a signal. Like, tap your head twice so I know when to laugh."

He let go of the scroll with one hand. The *snap* of its shutting caromed off the walls into the silence.

The dead silence.

Amy glanced around nervously. "Um, shouldn't there have been another train by now . . . ?"

Dan reached in his pockets. "I can't check. I think I dropped my schedule on the track."

"I mean, just logically—wouldn't another train have come through?" Amy said. "If not this direction, then the other? The trains are pretty frequent, right? Why is it so quiet?"

Alistair stood bolt upright. "Point taken. They must have closed down the power. Which means—"

The distant thrum of voices now filtered in through the walls. It was coming from the north, from the track on the side opposite the one they'd used.

"Who's that?" Dan asked. "Police?"

Alistair's face suddenly looked aged and puckered. "No," he replied, his voice shaky. *"Yakuza."*

"What do we do?" Dan asked.

"They can't find us, right?" Amy said. "So we stay?"

Alistair took Dan and Amy by the arm, pushing them toward the door. "They will eventually cross the tracks, see the lost shoe, the dropped schedule, the smudges worn off the wall plate. We must go."

"Cube!" Amy blurted, suddenly breaking loose and racing back to the pile. "Look! Sphere! Cylinder! Para — parallelowhatever! Those are geometric shapes — right, Dan? *They're right here!*"

Dan was already grabbing the globe, stuffing it into his backpack. "Take them all!"

"Quickly!" Alistair said. He took a small cube in one hand, a triangulated tube in another. Amy scooped up the long cylinder and headed back to the door.

In a moment, they were out on the track again. Alistair pushed the thick door closed behind him. Where a seamless, grime-darkened wall once stood, there was now the faint outline of a recently opened door.

The train that had almost hit them was now stopped beyond them, its rear cars not yet having reached the next station platform.

Amy pulled her shoe from under the rail and jammed it on her foot. She stumbled, her ankle throbbing with pain. But the thought of stopping petrified her. Clenching her teeth, she ran. They flew down the track, back in the direction they'd come. The station soon came into view, but the track was dotted with flashlights, beams moving around like fireflies.

They all stopped, their ragged breaths echoing in the tunnel.

"Police," Alistair whispered. "We cannot let them find us. They will arrest us."

The lights were getting closer, the voices louder. From the other side, it sounded as if the *yakuza* had switched over — to their side of the tracks.

"And the *yakuza*?" Dan asked.

"They'll kill us," Alistair replied.

"That's a no-brainer," Dan said, heading toward the cops.

"No!" Amy grabbed him by the arm.

"Where do *you* suggest we go?" Dan hissed.

Amy looked up. The bottom rung of a ladder hung just above her head.

"We must take the objects," Alistair said. He quickly removed his silk jacket, laid it flat, placed the objects on top, then gathered the jacket edges upward. Dan took a rope from his backpack and tied a knot, making a secure container.

Amy was already climbing, grimacing against the pain. Dan put the other end of the rope between his teeth, grabbed the ladder, and pulled himself up.

Below him, Alistair was gawking into the darkness, one hand on the ladder and the other clutching his walking stick. "Come on!" Dan shouted through his teeth.

"Just *go!*" Alistair cried.

Footsteps thudded against the track. A man appeared out of the darkness, his soot-covered face allowing only his teeth and eyes to pick up the light — until Dan noticed the gleam of a dagger in his right hand.

Now Alistair was moving. He was on the second rung when a guttural shriek rang out. *"HEEE-YAHHHHH!"*

Dan looked down to see the *yakuza* blade slicing through the air — at Uncle Alistair's legs.

CHAPTER 8

"Watch out!" Amy screamed.

"Hunh!" Alistair gasped, heaving himself upward.

Clanggggg!

Dan felt the ladder jolt. He hung on tight, staring at the amazing sight below.

With a sharp, precise movement, Alistair had brought his walking stick down hard, knocking the blade from the attacker's hand. Then, on the backswing, Alistair caught the *yakuza* on the side of the head, sending him spinning downward to the track.

"Get out, Dan!" Alistair commanded, shouting upward.

"How did you learn to do *that*?" Dan asked.

"I'm full of surprises — now *move*!" Alistair said.

Amy had managed to push aside the grating at the top of the ladder. Dan scrambled to the street, pulling up the objects behind him. A moment later, with a loud grunt, Alistair heaved himself up onto the sidewalk. A mother pushing a baby in a stroller swerved around them. Dan quickly began shoving the grating back, getting it over three-quarters of the hole before Alistair yanked him away.

"No time for that!" he said, pulling Dan with him as he stepped into the street.

"Wait!" Dan protested. "What about Amy?"

Amy was trying to catch up, limping over the curb in their direction.

Shiiiink . . . SHIIIINK!

Soot-stained fingers, reaching up from underground, were sliding the grate open.

"Pardon me, please," Alistair said, rushing over to the hole. Like a golf pro, he drew back his walking stick and swung it down toward the fingers. Hard.

"AAAAAAAGHHH!" came a tortured shout.

Dan heard the thumping of multiple bodies hitting the ground below the ladder.

Alistair knelt, his back to Amy. "Climb on."

She leaped onto him and he locked his arms under her knees, grimacing as he limped across the street behind Dan. Their shadows were elongated in the setting sun, making them look like some misshapen beast.

HONNNNK!

A car swerved out of the way, its driver shouting at them.

"The objects —" Alistair called out through gritted teeth. "Drop them in that alleyway. We will come back for them!"

Dan spotted a dark, narrow space between buildings and threw Alistair's tightly packed jacket into it.

They raced around the corner, up a hill between low brick buildings where the smell of soy sauce and fried shrimp belched out of ground-floor windows in steamy wisps. Alistair darted right at the top of the hill, into the open gate at the back of a vast, empty playground. "Where are we going?" Dan cried out.

"I have friends!" Alistair said. "All we need to do is get a taxi —"

As if by magic, a cab sped toward them up the street. Alistair let go of Amy with one hand and waved frantically, shouting in Japanese.

But as the taxi swerved at him, it picked up speed, its engine roaring.

"Look out!" Dan screamed.

Alistair jumped away. Amy went flying off onto the blacktop as the cab hopped the curb, missing them by an inch. It squealed to a stop and spun around.

At once, all four doors opened.

"Yakuza!" Alistair shouted.

Now even Amy was moving fast. As Dan ran after her, he heard a high whistling sound. "DUCK, AMY!"

A jagged-edged silver metal disk sliced the air. It whizzed over Dan's head as he leaped for his sister, grabbing her by the waist.

She screamed as they tumbled to the ground again.

"What was that?" Amy gasped.

"A shuriken," Dan shouted. "A ninja throwing star!"

"This way!" Alistair cried out. Dan felt the old man's hand clasp his wrist, yanking him upward. In a split second they were racing into a large steel tunnel, part of the playground.

Thunk! Thunk! Thunk-thunk-thunk-thunk-thunk!

Dan flinched as each throwing star hit the outside of the tunnel, inches from their heads.

They emerged from the other end into a complex of thick wooden climbing equipment. Alistair was running, crouched, his head low and his walking stick tucked under his arm. Splinters flew around their heads like hailstones.

Barking, angry Japanese instructions rang out behind them. Car doors slammed. Tires screeched. Dan, Amy, and Alistair ran blindly out of the playground, across a lawn, into a backyard, over a small fence. *"Yeowww!"* Amy shouted, her foot jamming in the fence's links.

"Keep up!" Alistair retorted.

The throwing stars had stopped, Dan realized. The *yakuza* wouldn't use them in a residential neighborhood—would they?

They emerged at the other end of a block, this one with a line of stores on either side. To their right, Dan could hear a speeding engine. "Go left!"

The street sloped downward to a big, open market area. Inside, vendors were packing up, cleaning out stalls. Dan realized that he, Amy, and Alistair could get safely lost in there. The *yakuza* would be asking for chaos if they followed.

VRRROOOOOM!

Dan stopped in his tracks. A red Porsche was turning into the road in front of them. Blocking their way to the market. Rounding the corner, the Porsche flashed its brights. Dan cowered, momentarily blinded.

Grabbing his sister, he sprang away from the street. "Jump—*jump*!"

They leaped onto the sidewalk, rolling past a metal mailbox as odd noises rang out. *Thwip! Thwip-thwip!*

Shots flew by them, up the hill from the Porsche to where the *yakuza* taxi was now bearing down on them.

Smash!

One of the taxi's headlights popped.

Thwip-thwip!

A projectile cracked the taxi's windshield. The taxi began to skid to the left, whirling. Its tires hopped the curb—and the car's broad left side hurtled toward Dan, Amy, and Alistair.

Amy screamed. Or maybe it was Dan himself. He couldn't tell. He was only aware of flying through the air. His head banged against the side of the building as a flash of yellow steel rolled by him, massive and dented.

With a sickening crunch, the taxi crashed through the plate glass window of a closed flower shop.

It came to rest on a bed of broken bouquets and shattered glass, its wheels in the air. Two men groggily worked their way out of the wreck, stumbling for a few seconds while they gained their bearing. Dan, Amy, and Alistair huddled together in the shadows, but the men ran up the hill, looking in dazed fear over their shoulder.

"What just happened?" Amy said.

"We were in a ninja fight," Dan said in amazement. "For the first time in my nonvirtual life. And I hated it."

A din of voices swelled from below as people from the market began walking up the hill to join the other gawkers, who descended from all sides.

Dan slowly stood. The Porsche was partially blocked from view by the mailbox, but Dan could see its gleaming mag wheels and tinted windows. "If they hadn't saved our butts . . . "

"Be careful," Alistair warned.

Suddenly, Dan heard the doors fly open. He froze.

"Mrrp?"

The tiny cry rang out. Dan's heart thumped as a silky animal grazed his ankle, and he glanced down at an Egyptian Mau that looked identical to Saladin but for the slightly mangy coat.

"Oh . . . " Amy said with a wistful smile.

"That looks just like you-know-who," Dan said.

The Mau was slinking over to Amy, who held out her arms to it.

"The breed is very popular around here," Alistair replied absently, his eyes still riveted on the Porsche. "Is anyone . . . alive in there?"

In reply, a figure staggered around from behind the mailbox. Dan's breath caught in his throat.

"Next time, dudes, hold on to your tickets," said Nellie Gomez.

CHAPTER 9

Dan gaped, ignoring his sister, who opened and closed her mouth in a stunning imitation of a spotted blowfish.

"*Mrrp?*" said Saladin.

"*Awwwweso-o-o-o-ome!*" Dan didn't care who heard him scream. He scooped up Saladin and threw his arms around Nellie.

Amy looked as if she'd just seen a ghost. But to Dan, Nellie felt real, all right. She felt all . . . spiky and leathery. And a split second later, Amy was all over her, too. Sobbing of course. Which made Nellie sob, too. Which almost ruined the whole thing. Even Alistair was a little teary.

Saladin climbed into Amy's arms, and she smiled disbelievingly. "But how did you . . . ?"

"Find you?" Nellie laughed. "It was all over the news—subway shut down, people on the tracks . . . I'm, like, *ding*! Amy and Dan, no-brainer!"

"Where'd you get the cool car?" Dan added.

"Where did those shots come from?" Amy asked.

"Where's the duffel?" Dan prodded.

"How did you escape the Kabras?" Alistair said.

"Whoa, whoa, whoa," Nellie said with a laugh. "I need backup!"

Behind her, two shadowy figures stepped out of the car. "She didn't escape us," said Ian Kabra.

"Far frub it," said Natalie in a stuffed-up voice.

Dan felt his blood run down to his feet. Amy gripped his arm.

"We just survived a ninja attack," Dan reminded her. "Remember, there are two of them and four of us."

"Mrrp," said Saladin.

"Sorry, five," whispered Dan.

"Ah-*chooo!*" Natalie sneezed. "I hate cats."

"ATTACK!" Dan yelled.

Ian grinned patiently at him—and brandished a sleek stun gun.

"Dan—duck!" Amy screamed.

"You asked about the shots?" Ian said. "This is your answer. You survived the *yakuza* because of my handling of this weapon. And because I insisted on renting a swift precision car, *not* the beige Chevy Cobalt your babysitter wanted."

"Id case you dod't udderstadt, you borons, we saved you," Natalie said. "Ah-*chooo!*"

"But . . . why?" Dan said. "You hate us."

"Dat's true." Natalie exhaled wearily.

"Yo, Nat? Take your allergy meds, okay, so you're not spraying me in the car?" Smiling at Dan and

Amy, Nellie grabbed the driver's door handle. "Get in, all of you."

"But—" Amy said, glancing reluctantly toward the Kabras.

"We have to move before the *yakuza* return," Nellie said. "I'll explain everything. Oh. And we squeezed your duffels in the trunk."

Yes! Dan thought. That meant they had the swords. Dan climbed into the soft leather backseat with Amy and Ian as the others squeezed into the front. "Whoa, *this* is street cred," Dan said. "Can we keep it?"

"We left some . . . outer clothing near the subway station," Alistair said carefully. "Perhaps I can direct you there, Nellie."

"Seat belts!" Nellie commanded. She started the car, pulled away from the curb, and floored it to get through a yellow light. Alistair pointed her to the right as she continued: "Okay, update. When I see Poindexter and Morticia on the plane? I freak. I'm, like, what happened to my kids? I think, they've, like, *eaten* you. Then they tell me what happened. *Bragging.* They're, like, fourteen and eleven, but they talk like they escaped from a Clue game. 'Forged the tickets, ho-ho!'— Anyway, they try to threaten me, yada yada, and of course I argue and I'm figuring in my head, 'Ha-ha, the next thing is they put poison in the drink'—but I'm, like, 'Nahh, of course they're not *that* skeezy.' Then I see her actually doing it, like *two inches away from me*—uh, hello? So I get kinda mad—you know, act like I'm going to drink it, and then *zam,* I spritz the stuff all over their faces. Well, I'm, like, 'Nyah nyah, this is really funny,' but they start to totally wig out and fall all over each other to get to their carry-on—they're, like, *'Eek our faces have schmutz on them!'* And I'm, like, *'Dudes, grow up!'* So I take their carry-on and sit on it. Um. Baad idea."

"The poison was in a concentrated form," Ian spoke up. "In the amount that Natalie had used, it would have mutilated, perhaps blinded us."

Amy squirmed away from him in disgust, nearly squeezing Dan into the side of the car. "And you were going to let Nellie *drink* it?" she said.

"We meant to temporarily disable her," Ian said. "Just a drop. But Natalie slipped during air turbulence. Before we could warn your nose-ringed nanny, she drenched us. Luckily, she allowed us to retrieve the antidote from our carry-on."

"That's kindness," Amy said.

"I made them agree to give me all their cash," Nellie explained.

"That's bribery," Natalie grumbled.

Nellie jerked the car to the right, and Dan felt like he was going to carry an Amy imprint on him for the rest of his life. Out of the corner of his eye, he saw Amy's hand brush accidentally against Ian's. She let out a yelp and pulled it away.

"Mrrp!" said Saladin, arching his back and spitting at Ian.

"Er, ahem," Ian said, leaning away from the cat, "the reason we are still here is that we'd like to propose a temporary alliance. As we explained to your porcine au pair, we have something you need."

"Like, two plane tickets?" Dan said. "Too late. And we'd rather have an alliance with a bucket of slime than with a Kabra—if we could tell the two things apart."

"Fine," Ian said. "We will use our artifact to find the clue ourselves—"

Alistair turned around toward Ian. "Artifact?"

"How refreshing, an open mind," Ian said with a sly smile. "As you well know, Mr. Oh, the Lucians have been collecting hints for years. So have the Ekats. And presumably so have . . . er, what branch *do* you belong to, Daniel?"

"The Cahills," Dan snapped. He hated that he and Amy were the only ones who didn't know their branch. "And you're crazy to think we'll work with you."

"Dan, they saved our lives," Amy said.

"They also tried to kill us!" Dan countered. "In the cave-in at Salzburg, in the canals of Venice—"

"There—you see how things change?" Natalie said brightly.

"Our . . . item once belonged to a Japanese warrior," Ian said. "It will be crucial for finding the next clue. Alas, neither Natalie nor I understand Japanese. Which is where you, Mr. Oh, come in." He leaned closer to the front seat. "You give us what you know. We'll give you what we have. We'll work together."

"Just for this one clue," Natalie quickly added. "Afterward, we cut you loose. We have our reputation to think of."

"Stop here," Alistair said to Nellie.

Screeeee! The Porsche squealed to a stop at a desolate corner.

"How do I know we can trust you?" Alistair demanded.

"W-we already know we c-c-can't," Amy said.

Ian grinned, reaching into his pocket. He pulled out a small velour bag stamped with the Kabra coat of arms and placed it in Amy's left hand. "This is yours, Amy Cahill. Now . . . how do we know we can trust *you*?"

A coin.

A stupid gold coin with a symbol on it—that's how the Kabras were buying their trust. Alistair had read the Japanese print on the back and claimed it might have belonged to Hideyoshi—*might*. Dan couldn't stand it. Collaborating with the Kabras was like kissing your sister. Well, maybe not that bad.

"The coin is so beautiful," Amy whispered, as they rounded the corner toward the alleyway where Dan had tossed the objects. Just ahead of them, Uncle Alistair was filling in Ian and Natalie on what had happened in the subway.

"It's a token for the arcade games at Laser Sport Time!" Dan hissed.

"Uncle Alistair doesn't think so," Amy murmured. "He's a numismatist."

"He takes his clothes off in public?" Dan said.

"It means *coin collector*! Besides, I sense Ian's telling the truth."

"That's because he touched your hand and did a mind meld."

"Shhh!" Amy said, as Ian glanced toward them.

The late-afternoon sky was a bruised purple as they reached the alleyway across from the subway stop. The silk jacket was still in the corner like a discarded old bag. Despite the near darkness, Dan could read the familiar look on Amy's face.

Sorry to embarrass you in front of your boyfriend, he thought.

Alistair knelt to pick up the cube container. "Move quickly," he said.

With a reluctant sigh, Dan struggled to remove the rusted top from the cylindrical container. Beside him, Alistair flung aside the cube with disgust. "Nothing in here but lizards."

As he reached for another container, a long black car pulled to a stop across the street. A black-uniformed man got out of the driver's seat and ran around to open the passenger door.

Dan crept forward in the shadows to watch. An Asian man, rail-thin and elderly, climbed out. His silver-white hair flowed past his shoulders, and he was dressed in an elegant dark suit with a silk pocket handkerchief. Walking along the sidewalk, he flipped open a cell phone as he knelt by the subway opening and peered inside.

Dan tapped Amy on the shoulder.

He heard Uncle Alistair let out a gasp and mutter something under his breath that sounded like "Bye."

"Bye?" Dan said, as Alistair suddenly pulled him farther into the shadow.

The old man headed back into the car, and it quickly drove out of sight.

"Who was that?" Dan asked. "The king of the *yakuza*?"

"We . . . " Alistair's voice seemed to catch in his throat. "We need to hurry. Open all the containers. *Now.*"

With a grunt, Dan finally managed to yank the top off the cylinder, releasing a stream of nuts, bolts, screws, and rivets.

"Fascinating . . . " Ian spilled tools from the rectangular box. "I adore hammers."

Alistair exhaled with frustration. "That room we

found may have been a subway storage facility sealed off during construction years ago and forgotten."

"But what kind of subway workers leave mysterious haikus?" Amy asked, tentatively prying the top off the triangular-shaped tube.

"Maybe they're really songs," Dan said with a weary smile. "'Cause, you know, those guys work on *tracks* all day. . . ."

"Hey, look!" Amy moved into the streetlamp light, pulling a long scroll out of the tube. As the others gathered around, Dan trained his flashlight on the text at the center. It was written in dark, elegant calligraphy, surrounded by a faded, unfinished-looking landscape of a rock outcropping and hills.

Alistair began translating: "'In the place of the final conquest, between three horns lies the people's wealth. And by the elements united is entrance granted, the highest to be revealed.'"

"Clear as wasabi," Dan remarked.

"Those letters right below," Amy said. "They look . . . *English.*"

Dan grabbed the flashlight from his backpack and beamed it on a group of plain, thickly drawn letters at the bottom of the scroll:

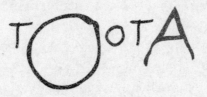

"Toota?" Ian said. "Could it be a phonetic spelling of the French *toute*?"

"Good, Ian, good," Dan said. "*French*, on a Japanese scroll."

"'Final conquest' . . . " Alistair murmured. "That's it! That's the key. I know where the clue is!"

"Where?" Amy and Dan asked at the same time.

A smile crossed Alistair's face for the first time all day. "The place where Hideyoshi mounted his final campaign and suffered his most humiliating defeat!"

"Right," Ian said uncertainly. "Of course. And . . . that would be . . . ?"

"We are going home," Alistair said, his eyes ablaze. "To Korea."

CHAPTER 10

Bae.

The name, once so important in his life, now consumed Alistair with rage.

His uncle Bae had been so close. Across the street!

It wasn't the right time, Alistair reminded himself. He would have to wait. To plan.

He turned in his seat to check on his flight companions. The Kabra siblings were absorbed in an old episode of *The O.C.* on their personalized seat-back flight screens, and the Cahills were doing the airline magazine crossword puzzle.

Quietly, he unfolded the printout from the library. In his lifetime, Alistair had spent a fortune on private investigators looking for the man who had taken everything from him. Now the man's identity had been discovered. He had died of old age—a respectable elder who had secretly built his fortune on contract killings and kept a record of each one in a private vault. Apparently, he had kept everything.

Alistair spread the printout on his tray table. Fingers shaking, he read it for what seemed like the hundredth time:

RETRIEVED, H. H. KOH INVESTIGATIONS, AUG. 25 01:23:52
UPLOADED VPN AUG. 25 03:14:27

OH INDUSTRIES

April 22, 1948

Dear ▓▓▓▓▓▓▓

     Brother will be arriving on 15:07 Delta flight, Idlewild Airport in New York, May 11. Booked into Room 1501 at Waldorf Astoria on Park Avenue. Scheduled to meet car in front of hotel on May 12 at 7:15 P.M., after dinner, for trip to Broadway play at Imperial Theater. Driver is ▓▓▓▓▓▓▓. Will take route across 45th Street.

     Upon completion of mission, payment will be forwarded by the expected means. Please confirm $5K US as proper amount. Destroy letter immediately.

Sincerely,

Bae Oh

Bae Oh
Senior Vice President

Alistair forced himself to read it, fighting back nausea and anger.

Five thousand dollars.

His father's life for five thousand dollars.

The details of what had happened in New York were hardwired into Alistair's brain. He still carried around with him the tattered, yellow news clipping of the murder: *New York City, May 12, 1948: Korean industrialist Gordon Oh was killed at the intersection of Madison Avenue and 45th Street while being driven to the theater.*

Here is what the newspapers all said: There had been a break-in at Brooks Brothers, an alarm, the desperate robber running up the avenue with a gun and trying to commandeer a car stopped at a red light— his father's hired limousine. Mr. Oh had tried to subdue the man. He had struggled nobly but tragically lost his life. The gunman had slipped away and was never found.

His dad had been in the wrong place at the wrong time. An unlucky accident.

That was the official report.

As a child, Alistair had never suspected foul play. But sometimes accidents were planned, and killers were hired. He had always been afraid of his uncle Bae Oh, his father's twin brother. Bae had grown up the lazy twin, the greedy slacker, repeatedly passed over for the head of the Ekaterina family, always under the shadow of the robust and well-loved Gordon. As an adult, Bae was all about foul play, as ruthless as a Kabra in his business dealings.

Bae craved glory and riches—and the 39 Clues. Whoever stood in his way had to go. Even his own brother.

It didn't matter that Gordon had a wife halfway across the world whose grief was so great that she needed to be hospitalized. Or a four-year-old boy whose heart that day had been ripped out.

A boy who was packed off, crying and alone, to be brought up by a man with a heart of glass, to be ignored and mocked his whole life.

His uncle Bae Oh. The murderer's boss.

Alistair glanced at the Cahill children. They were squabbling over the answer to a crossword puzzle now, the argument turning into a joke, the boy making up a nonsense word — a babble of nonsense words, a burst of laughter. Even now they sounded as they did eleven years ago, as a newborn and a three-year-old. Back when Alistair had made his promise to Hope and Arthur. A promise that had been nearly impossible to keep.

The children wouldn't remember, of course. But he did. And now the couple was gone, for the same reason he'd lost his own parents. For the Clues.

He sighed. At least the children had each other.

All Alistair could hope for was revenge.

His fingers shook as he folded the sheet and put it back into his pocket. On this flight, he knew he would not sleep.

CHAPTER 11

Rumor had it that Alistair Oh was broke. His business had not succeeded. But when Amy saw his mansion, in a village outside Seoul, South Korea, she began pondering recipes for cheesy burrito fillings.

"Dang! Whose palace?" Nellie blurted, as the limo pulled to a stop after their brief drive from the airport.

A pristine white building stood gleaming atop a sloping, luxuriant lawn. The front path was decorated with orange and yellow chrysanthemums and led to a small grove of cherry trees and dogwoods, their leaves rustling in the breeze. Just being here, in this setting, made you want to smile.

"Where is the main house?" asked Natalie, as they climbed out.

"Voilà." Alistair gestured dully toward the mansion. All day long he had seemed tired to Amy, a little off his game.

"You mean, behind the pool house?" said Natalie.

Ian elbowed her in the ribs.

"My home is one of the few remaining perks from my days as a burrito magnate," Alistair said, as he walked up the drive. He was flanked by the Kabras and the driver, who held Dan and Amy's bags. "As is Mr. Chung, my driver. And Harold, my butler. Our cozy little team. Things used to be a bit more grand."

"Ah, well, easy come, easy go — not that I actually know the feeling," Ian replied. "The house does have lovely . . . um, window moldings."

"Thank you, they were imported from South America," Alistair replied.

Dan leaned into his sister as they followed behind the others. *"Window moldings?"* he muttered. "What normal fourteen-year-old guy talks about window moldings?"

Amy shrugged. "Did you check the duffel?" she whispered.

"Yes," Dan replied. "Rufus and Remus are still there."

Amy took off her shoes and stepped onto the soft, freshly cut grass. A cool breeze tickled her nose and she burst out laughing, windmilling her arms as she spun in the grass on her good ankle.

"Oh, great, I'm in South Korea and my sister has turned into Julie Andrews," Dan said.

Oops.

Amy dropped her arms. Now everyone was ogling her. She felt like she did in ballet class. Dumpy and uncoordinated and ugly. She glanced down into the clover, as if by staring hard enough she would disappear inside it.

"What your sister is doing," Ian said, walking toward the house, "is called *enjoying herself*. Maybe you could learn from her, Daniel. It's refreshing."

"Refreshing?" Dan said. *"Amy?"*

Amy stuck her tongue out at her brother. Ian was smiling at her, which made her stomach churn, but she managed a smile back. Just to get on Dan's nerves.

She stayed a few steps behind Ian as they crested the hill, until Amy could see the back of Alistair's house. It extended to a large sundeck overlooking a swimming pool and a vast lawn. To one side of the lawn, a stream wound its way through a landscaped rock garden that contained a pond stocked with goldfish. To the other side was a thick hedgerow that seemed to go on forever.

"Tempting Tempura microwavable burritos bought me this," Alistair said, gesturing over the landscape. "Mostly beef."

"Tranquil." Natalie nodded. "It really is amazing what you can do with a limited amount of space."

Alistair raised an eyebrow. "Nothing like the Kabra estate, I hear."

"We hated growing up there," Ian replied. "Every year one of us would get lost on the lush grounds, and they would have to send the homing poodles after us."

"The *what*?" Dan said.

Natalie sighed ruefully. "Some say it was an abusive childhood, but we didn't know any better."

Nellie emerged from the house. Behind her was a uniformed butler with six soft drink bottles, which he set on a table next to six wooden chairs. "Thank you, Harold," Alistair said as the butler bowed and went back inside. "If Toyotomi Hideyoshi had had his way, this land would be Japanese. He intended to conquer all of East Asia, and he had never failed. Some say he meant to build his grandest palace here in Korea, to give birth to an heir who would take over the kingdom. He would also build great vaults and hiding places. Hideyoshi was one of history's most notorious collectors—"

"I knew I liked the guy!" said Dan.

"According to family lore, he collected the most valuable item of all," Alistair said. "One of the clues to the Cahill family secret, which we still seek five centuries later." He sighed. "No Ekat has ever found it. No one suspected it was in Korea. But our parchment will lead us there, if we know how to read it."

"Dude, I'm on it," Dan said. "How do we get started?"

"Unfortunately," Alistair said with a yawn, "I cannot function after a rough, sleepless flight. Will you kindly grant an old man a half-hour nap in his own bed? Harold will feed you until then. Please stay close by and do not wander."

"Of course," Amy said.

Alistair waved to them and walked into the house.

"Food, drink, magazines, TV, TiVo, Internet, hand-held devices?" Harold asked.

"Warcraft?" Dan blurted.

Harold smiled. "Second door on the right."

As Dan scooted inside, Natalie settled into a lounge chair with the Korean edition of *People* magazine and Nellie worked her iPod.

Ian was staring out into the yard. "What's that?" he asked.

"Wh-wh-what's what?" Amy said.

He pointed to a dense hedgerow that contained a narrow gap. "Is it a hedge maze? Come on, let's go and look."

"I—I don't think so."

"Why not?" Ian said. "What else are we going to do?"

He had this funny look on his face, Amy thought. A curious smile, as if she had just refused an ice cream sundae or the winnings to the lottery. Like it wouldn't have occurred to him that anyone could possibly say no.

"Alistair t-told us not to wander," she explained, shoving her hands in her pockets.

Ian cocked his head teasingly. "I thought you were a brave explorer."

"Oh, p-p-please . . . " Amy said, trying to drip with sarcasm but fighting the tingle that was spreading up from the back of her neck.

"Well," he said with a shrug. "Your choice."

As he walked away, Amy lurched forward but stopped herself.

What am I doing? she thought.

He was a jerk. He was jerkier than a jerk. He was a new definition for jerk. She didn't have to follow him.

Her fingers closed around the coin he had given her. She pulled it out of her pocket and flipped it in the air. "Heads I f-f-follow, tails I stay."

The coin landed with the odd symbol facing upward. But was that a head or a tail?

Ian sighed disappointedly. "Ah, well, my loss . . . "

As his hair, glinting in the sun, disappeared beyond the hedgerow, she turned and trudged into the house.

◦———⟨◦⟩———◦

"AAAAGGHHHHH!"

At the sound of the scream, Alistair barged barefoot out of his room. He raced past Amy, who was being served orange juice in the kitchen.

She followed him outside, with Harold and Dan close behind.

In the distance, Amy heard a violent growl, a rustling from the hedges. Ian burst out of the opening, one shoe missing, running at top speed. "HELLLLLP!"

Behind him was an enormous dog, a mutt that seemed to be part pit bull, part Great Dane, and from the looks of it, possibly part black bear.

"What the—?" Alistair said. "STOP! SIT!"

"I can't sit! He bit me on the bum!" Ian shrieked.

"Really?" Nellie said, grinning.

Alistair was limping onto the lawn now, waving his finger at the beast, which hung its head sheepishly and whimpered. "Is this how you greet me on my return, you naughty thing?" Alistair scolded. "Bad dog! Bad, *bad* Buffy!"

"*Buffy?*" Dan said.

GRRRRRRR.

"Shhh, she's sensitive about her name," Alistair replied.

"*I'll sue!*" Ian sputtered. "*I'll sue you AND the dog. And the country of South Korea. And . . . and . . .*"

"The landscape architect?" Natalie said.

"*The landscape architect!*" Ian shouted.

"Buffy is actually a real pussycat," Alistair said, eyeing Ian suspiciously, "unless you surprise her."

"*Flowrf! Flowrf!*" barked Buffy, throwing a spray of saliva left and right.

"She is sooooo cute!" Nellie said.

"*These are handsewn Persian silk!*" Ian turned around, revealing a tear in his pants that exposed boxers with pink dollar signs on a white background, then quickly spun back around. "Uh, never mind."

"Sweeet," Nellie said.

"Shut up," Natalie snapped, barely stifling a laugh herself.

"I fail to find the humor in this!" Ian shouted, his eyes red with rage and embarrassment. "And neither will you. I will drain you, Alistair. I will bring you to your knees—"

"Young man," Alistair interrupted sharply, "I am too old and too wise to be intimidated by a fourteen-year-old boy who wakes me from a much-needed sleep by his foolish actions. Why were you snooping in my hedges when I told you not to?"

"Who ever heard of planting a guard dog in the middle of a hedge maze?" Ian snapped back. "What is back there, Alistair? What are you hiding?"

Alistair cleared his throat. Pulling a comb from a pocket, he tidied his hair as if he were about to go to a business meeting. "I suppose," he said, "we will have to do this now. Perhaps, Mr. Kabra, you would like to change." He called over his shoulder. "Harold, please apply some disinfectant to the young man's wounds."

Ian went pale. "I'll do it myself," he said, heading into the house.

Nellie flopped back in a lounge chair, her face covered with sunscreen. "Wake me when it's over."

As they tramped through the hedge, Amy could see the hurt in Ian's eyes. He was wearing a pair of Harold's uniform pants now, which were a couple of sizes too large.

"These itch," Ian grumbled.

"No spare pants in your carry-on?" Dan said. "Bummer!"

Cackling, Dan scampered ahead. Ian turned toward Amy, trying valiantly to smile. "I meant, the bite marks itch. Not the trousers."

She fell in step beside him. "He—he—should have—" The harder she tried, the worse it felt. The words were like volleyballs stuck in her throat.

"Alistair should have warned me?" Ian said. "Thank you. My feelings exactly."

"Uh-huh," Amy replied. *Talk much?* she thought. She clutched her jade necklace, fiddling furiously with the chain.

"*You* warned me, though," Ian said softly. "I should have listened."

"Well, um . . . " Amy said, feeling suddenly as if the temperature had shot up ten degrees.

Ian laughed. "Oh, well. I suppose it will only hurt when I sit."

Amy fell into step beside him, watching his footfalls land on the grass, counting how many steps she took compared to his. He had a strong stride.

Before long, they reached the others. Alistair had stopped before a section of hedge and was groping around inside it.

Dan was glaring at Amy.

What was that about? his face said.

Dan glanced accusingly at Ian. Before he could glance back, Amy turned away.

She could read his mind anyway. She hated when he was right.

Alistair was now clearing a section of brush to reveal a door with a round, cast-iron hatch. The Kabras, the Cahills, and Buffy all gathered around gawking, except for Buffy, who drooled.

On the hatch was the number 5005. Beneath that was a heavy latch and a circular dial engraved with numbers from 1 to 30, like a combination lock.

"This, my children," Alistair said proudly, "was barbecue pork."

Dan rapped his fingers against the latch. "Been out in the sun a long time."

"I mean, sales of my barbecue pork burritos bought this," Alistair said. "The combination involves four numbers, and all the information you need to know is here. You get three tries. I can give you one hint—but that will use up a try."

Ian frowned. Amy could see the wheels turning in his head.

She took a deep breath. 5005. There was something about that number.

"The number is a palindrome," Ian said, "the same backward and forward. That may mean something."

"It's two-zero-zero-two upside down," offered Natalie.

Dan exhaled loudly. "Rich doesn't guarantee smart. It's, like, so obvious, dude."

"Pardon?" Ian said.

"Don't overthink—Uncle Alistair said we have everything we need to know!" He spun the numbers 5, 0, 0, and 5, and then pulled the latch.

Stuck solid.

"That was Try Number One," Alistair said.

Ian glanced at Dan. "Maybe thinking isn't such a bad idea."

"I think we need the hint," Natalie said.

"Very well," Alistair said. "It is a riddle: Why leave the factory when the workers are in their prime?"

The question hung in the air. Amy's mind raced.

"Prime . . . " Dan said, his face worked into a prunish mask of concentration. "Okay, what's the prime of someone's life? Like, twenty-one years old? Maybe one of the numbers is twenty-one!"

As he reached for the dial, Alistair said, "Remember, you have only one chance left. If you fail, I cannot let you in."

Dan's hand froze. "Come on, guys, help me out here. Twenty-one and . . . ?"

"Well, when does a worker leave a factory?" Ian said. "This, I'm afraid, is beyond the Kabra experience."

"Twelve noon for lunch?" Dan said. "And five o'clock to go home. So . . . twenty-one, twelve, and five?"

"No!" Amy blurted out. She wasn't sure, but the hint was a lot like the ones in the Puns and Anagrams puzzles that Dan used to do in the Sunday *New York Times*. The hint was partially hidden in the wording — you just needed to know how to read it. "Um, I think it's none of those. Can I try?"

Dan scowled at her. "Amy, *I'm* the puzzle guy. I'm all over this."

Amy shrank back. Maybe he was seeing something else. Dan always saw stuff no one else did. He was a genius at puzzles. He had solved an ancient code on a pile of skulls in the sewers of Paris. He had figured out the secret encoded in Mozart's sheet music.

But he was being distracted now. He was looking at Ian as if he wanted to kill him with optical lightsabers.

He wasn't thinking.

"I—I'm pretty sure I have this," Amy said.

Alistair grinned. He gestured to the dial. "Please."

Amy averted her eyes from the disbelieving glare of her brother. "Well, think about that phrase—'Why leave the factory.' 'Why' sounds like the letter Y. If the letter Y leaves the word *factory*, you're left with—"

"Factor!" Natalie announced.

"And the workers?" Amy said, reaching out to the latch. "They're 'in their *prime*'—"

"*Prime . . . factors?*" Dan said.

"So that would be the prime numbers that you multiply together to get five thousand and five . . . " Ian murmured. "Sounds a bit far-fetched?"

"I hate math," Natalie said.

Amy's hand shook as she carefully turned the dial. . . .

5, 7, 11, 13.

Click.

She turned the latch and pulled the hatch open.

"Welcome," Alistair said, "to the Oh sanctum."

CHAPTER 12

It's a small room, Ian thought, *but ugly*.

He smiled. An old Kabra family joke.

The Cahill brother—Dan—was gazing about the musty, wood-paneled room as if he were about to cry. "For this, you have a murderous, man-eating, killer beast?" he cried out. "To guard *a library*?"

Amy was looking about the sanctum in awe. "It's . . . beautiful!"

The girl was modest and thoughtful. How bizarre. So rarely did Ian see these qualities in others—especially during the quest for the 39 Clues. Naturally, he had been taught to avoid these behaviors at all costs and never to consort with anyone who possessed them. They were distasteful—FLO, as Papa would say. For Losers Only. And Kabras never lost.

Yet she fascinated him. Her joy in running up Alistair's tiny lawn, her awe at this piddling cubbyhole—it didn't seem possible to gain so much happiness from so little. This gave him a curious feeling he'd never quite experienced. Something like indigestion but quite a bit more pleasant.

Ah, well. Blame it on the ripped trousers, he thought. Humiliation softened the soul.

He glanced at the cramped shelves, the mildewed oak walls, the cracked leather armchair, the hideous fluorescent lights, the mouse droppings in the corners, the scuffed moldings, and the artwork that seemed to have been bought at a tag sale for the color-blind. *Beautiful?*

"It's books," Dan groaned. "Beam me up, Scotty—*please!*"

For once, Ian rather agreed with him.

"Rare books," Alistair said, gesturing grandly to a section of four glassed-in shelves, "not to mention one of the world's finest collections of secret material about the Cahill family. A lifelong passion for me, as few items were ever duplicated. Here is our best hope of decoding the parchment!"

Ian began to sit, but he thought of how that would make his posterior feel. Standing up wasn't pleasant, either, with the polyester trousers that felt like sandpaper on his legs. And Dan's whining just made the experience unbearable.

He would have to avoid the brother. The sister, at least, was interesting. He wondered if her lack of cynicism would be contagious.

How distasteful. Still . . .

"Perhaps we should form teams," Ian suggested. "A race. Amy and I will scour the material on the top two shelves, Natalie and Dan take the bottom two."

"Excellent," Alistair said. "Do you agree, Amy?"

"Um . . . " Amy said, her eyes darting away from him. "Uh . . . "

A pity, Ian thought. So many females had this reaction to him. It really did limit conversation.

"I've never been on an extra-Kabricular team before," Natalie said, smiling at her own wittiness. "But I'll try, I suppose."

Dan was staring at an expensive but unfortunate painting of a couple quite familiar to Ian. The man's hair was piled in mangled gray wisps, his eyebrows bushy and his eyes wild. The woman had a strong face, the way a horse was strong — long-jawed and big-eared. Above them floated all kinds of strange-looking symbols. "Who's the lucky couple?" Dan asked.

"Ah, yes, the ever-glamorous Gideon and Olivia, the original Cahills, painted in the early 1500s," Ian said. "Your ancestors."

"The Kabras improved the bloodline," Natalie said.

"Ready?" Alistair spread out the parchment on a table, then grabbed a book off the shelf. "I will help the younger team, Natalie and Dan. Set . . . go!"

Ian ran his fingers along the line of books, some with handwritten titles along the spines: *Historicus Cahilliensis: Ekaterina, Vols. I and II . . . Ekat Architectural Renderings . . . A Review of Eighteenth-Century Cahill Literature. . . .* Some of them seemed like pamphlets, notes torn from three-ring binders. It would be difficult to find anything helpful here.

Amy was pulling down a thick book titled *Origins of the Cahills: A Compendium of Contemporary Studies*.

"We're supposed to find a *clue,* not study history," Dan snapped.

"But we know so little about the Cahill family," Amy said.

Natalie looked up from a book she was skimming. "I don't know *why* your parents never told you which branch you were in. We knew the whole story before we were walking."

Ian watched Amy as her face sank. He felt a flutter inside. Sympathy, he realized — an emotion he often felt for the Kabra banker on days when the stock market performed badly. This feeling, however, was somehow a bit more . . . vivid.

He gave his sister a kick. "Natalie, have you lost your sense of . . . grace?"

She glared at him for a moment, until the joke clicked in.

"'The Cahill family traces back to early 1500s Dublin, with the brilliant, eccentric Gideon Cahill and his wife, Olivia,'" Amy read aloud.

Alistair nodded encouragingly. His niece was so excited she could barely get the words out.

" 'Some say Cahill had indeed made a discovery to change the course of humankind,'" Amy continued. " 'But the nature of this discovery was never known. In 1507, a sudden fire swept through the Cahill home. All escaped but one. Gideon, desperate to save his life's work, was found burned to death at his desk.'"

"What is it with Cahills and fire?" Dan whispered.

Alistair felt a little clutch in his chest. The children had been through so much tragedy—the fire that had trapped their parents, the one that had burned Grace's house. It occurred to him why he'd never wanted children of his own.

You risked caring for them. And that kind of feeling could be dangerous in the hunt for the 39 Clues.

" 'According to contemporary sources, at his death, Gideon had been studying the secrets of alchemy—the attempt to turn base metals into gold,'" Amy went on. " 'He sought a substance called the philosopher's stone. The problem was, the substance did not exist—yet. It was considered the key to the final quest. Being *more perfect* than gold, the stone, also known as alkahest, would be powerful enough to turn other substances into gold.'"

"Thank you, Ms. Frizzle," Dan said, furiously reading through a pile of pamphlets. "Keep going, but this time try *reading to yourself.*"

"Don't you all see?" Amy said, jumping out of her seat. "We've done it!"

"Done what?" Dan said.

Amy grabbed her brother and swung him around like she'd done when he was three. "Gideon *made* that 'discovery to change the course of humankind'! He cracked the secret of the philosopher's stone. *We've discovered the secret to the thirty-nine clues!*"

"What?" Ian said. "You figured out the parchment code? The clue?"

"No—something bigger than the clue," Amy said.

Natalie plopped angrily down into a chair. "Did we lose? I *hate* being on a team."

Alistair looked over Amy's shoulder, pushing aside the Kabras, who insisted on blocking his view. Amy flipped the page to a diagram of alchemical symbols:

Alchemy Chart

Fire Water Earth Air

Gold Sulphur Mercury Salt

Philosopher's Stone
(Alkahest)

Amy brought a coin out of her pocket. "The shape — the philospher's stone — it's on this coin!" she exclaimed.

"Cool," Dan replied. "But what's so big about that?"

"Don't you see?" Amy repeated. "This page is the secret to the whole thing — what the thirty-nine clues add up to!"

"So . . . when we collect all of them . . ." Dan said, a grin spreading slowly across his face.

"We will possess the secret to alchemy — the philospher's stone!" Amy put the coin back in her pocket and glanced at the book. "We'll find out how the coin fits in, too. But listen—

"'After the fire of 1507, Thomas and Kate fled Ireland for England, smuggling components of Gideon's work — which they vowed to continue. Thomas married and had a family but began neglecting his sister and their mission. The angry Katherine ran away, taking something of such importance that Thomas left everything to chase after her. After trying Paris, Venice, and Cairo, Thomas gave up. Attracted to the rough samurai culture, he settled in Japan, assuming a modest lifestyle. His youngest son, Hiyoshimaru, grew up to become Toyotomi Hideyoshi.'"

"The Bald Rat was the son of Thomas — *the* original Tomas?" Dan said. "That's promising."

Alistair cast a wary glance at the Kabras. He could read their parched, sarcastic faces — their impatience at the fact that Dan and Amy were learning things that the other teams had known for a long time. He knew they were struggling to wait out the Cahills' learning curve. After all, Dan and Amy had been very good at finding new Clues that had eluded the others.

And they were on to something here.

"Can't we skip past GO, collect two hundred dollars, and get to the parts we don't know yet?" Natalie said with a yawn.

"Get off your butt, Natalie, and let's keep looking," Dan said. "We're . . . thirty-seven clues away from the secret to alchemy!"

He swung around, shoving a book back into a shelf and reaching for another. A ragged old book, teetering on the shelf edge, fell to the floor.

Alistair cringed. "Careful, some of these are priceless!" he warned, bending to pick up the delicate book and examining the hand-drawn Japanese characters on the cover. "It's five centuries old. Found by an enemy warlord. It was the only item found in Hideyoshi's tent during a raid—"

"What's it say?" Dan asked.

Alistair adjusted his glasses. "The cover reads, 'Hideyoshi, nine'—perhaps a sketchbook or coloring book from his childhood."

"Wait, why would this even say 'Hideyoshi'?" Amy asked. "Wasn't he called something else as a child?"

Alistair's eyes widened. "Yes—Hiyoshimaru! Good catch. If this were really his childhood book, *that* would be the name on it."

Amy gently took the book. As she flipped through the pages—landscapes, battle scenes, monsters—the others gathered around her. Alistair noticed the Kabra boy gently touching her shoulder. "Th-th-this . . . this stuff is way too g-g-good for a nine-year-old . . ."

Hands shaking, his niece opened to a page that showed a strange, modern-looking jotting of stars and random lines. "A kid could have done that," Natalie said.

"'Hideyoshi . . . nine . . .'" Dan said. "Hey—this is *page* nine!"

Suddenly, without saying a word, Amy reached into the book and ripped the page out.

Alistair thought he would have a heart attack. "Amy!" he blurted. "This is an antique!"

Amy quickly leaned over his table, laying the ripped-out sheet on top of the parchment.

They fit together. Most of the lines made a detailed landscape of a rocky area. But other lines, tighter and smaller, seemed to form Korean characters.

And Alistair saw the method to the girl's madness. "The three horns . . . " he said.

"Say *what*?" Dan said.

"Ha-ha!" Alistair gave his niece a hug. She really was an extraordinary child. "Thanks to Amy, I know where this is. And we're going there first thing tomorrow morning."

CHAPTER 13

Somehow, on a bumpy morning car ride after an egg breakfast, Dan did not like thinking of the name Pukhansan. But that's where they were headed at the crack of dawn.

As they neared the city of Seoul, a three-peaked mountain loomed before them. "The three horns— I should have realized it from the beginning," Alistair said. "It is Samgaksan, the three peaks. The confusion is that it is now known by the name Pukhansan."

"*Glurp . . .*" Dan said, closing his eyes and sinking back into the seat and the oversize hooded Harvard sweatshirt Alistair had lent him.

Amy stared through the car window. The day was gray and gloomy, and the mountain looked nearly vertical. They had packed lunches in her backpack, but this was obviously going to be more than a day hike.

"We have to climb that?" Nellie asked. "I'm wearing Vans."

"Mountains have strong profiles," Natalie said, flicking a piece of dust off her pink jeweled Prada sneakers, which she had given to Harold to clean. "And so should we."

"It's only about a half mile high, but I do not think we will be climbing," Alistair replied, referring to the overlay of ancient parchment and sheet. "The old drawing has a solid meandering line through it, which I take to be the famous fortress wall. It cuts through several valleys and low-lying areas."

"What's this?" Dan said, pointing to a funny squiggly formation.

"Uh, an M," said Nellie. "Or if you look at it the other way, a W. Or sideways, kind of S-ish . . . "

"Maybe it's palm trees," Dan said. "Like in the movie *It's a Mad, Mad, Mad, Mad World*. You know? No? These guys need to find hidden money, and the only clue they have is it's under a big W? And no one sees what it means—but then, near the end of the movie, there's this grove of four palm trees rising up in the shape of . . . you-know-what! Classic!"

Amy, Alistair, Natalie, Ian, and Nellie all looked at him blankly.

"There is no W in the Korean language," Alistair replied. "Or palm trees in Korea. It might be maple trees . . . "

"*Mrrp,*" said Saladin, rubbing his face against Dan's knee.

"I'll tell you the rest of the plot later," Dan whispered to the Mau.

Alistair's driver let them off in the parking lot of Pukhansan National Park. A crowd of tourists had gathered around a giant trail map, which Alistair carefully compared to his parchment-sheet overlay. He traced the dark snaky line with his finger, stopping at various black marks. "These, I presume, are ancient temples. Let's assume the big X is our hidden treasure—"

"It's between two of the temples," Natalie said. "But which two?"

Alistair shrugged heavily. "There are many of them. And much space between them. This may take several days."

"Then let's go!" Dan said.

"Someone has to stay here with Saladin and Mr. Chung," Nellie piped up, giving the mountain a dubious glance. "Okay, you talked me into it; I will."

The rest of them took off down a well-beaten pathway. "Hideyoshi conquered most of what is now South Korea," said Alistair, "including Seoul, which was then called Hanseong. But the soldiers put up a fight, building this fortress wall to ward off the invasion."

"Why would Hideyoshi bury his treasures here?" Amy asked.

Alistair shrugged. "To use the wall's protection, perhaps. He assumed this would remain his territory."

"Overconfidence is a curse," Ian remarked.

"You would know," Dan said.

As the path climbed, there were fewer and fewer hikers. Each time they passed a temple, Alistair checked the overlay, each time shaking his head.

His back was coated with sweat now, and he was panting as he finally sat on a rock ledge. "Lunchtime," he announced, handing the overlay to Amy. "My dear, would you kindly keep this in your backpack?"

"Lunch? We're just getting started!" Ian said, scampering up the wall, his loose Harold pants ballooning in the breeze.

Natalie sat eagerly next to Alistair. "You didn't happen to bring prosciutto with buffalo mozzarella and sun-dried tomatoes on whole-grain focaccia with pesto sauce?"

"Peanut butter and banana on white?" Dan offered.

Alistair was intent on the surroundings. "I fear we may have missed the spot. The wall may have been repositioned over the centuries. It may not look like this anymore."

As Amy zipped her pack shut, she felt something hit the top of her head—a clump of moss, which bounced off and landed at her feet. "Hey!"

Ian was laughing as he wiped the dirt off his hands.

Laughing. Not to mention staring at her. His eyes were mocking, pinning her in place. As if planning some snarky Kabra comment. In front of everybody.

She fought back tears, fighting the urge to run back or curl into a shell.

"Throw it back," Dan hissed. "Hard!"

Ian cupped his hand to his mouth. "Amy, will you accept a challenge? A race to the top of the next big rock? I'll give you a head start—or are you too slow?"

"She's not slow!" Dan shouted back. "Well, actually, she is."

Amy stood up. It was one thing to be humiliated by a Kabra, but not by a snot-nosed little brother.

She eyed the big rock. This was insane. He was baiting her, setting her up for more embarrassment. Unless . . .

There it was. Another path through the brush. More direct.

She started to run.

"Amy—leave your backpack!" Dan called out. "And remember to name your first child after me!"

She ignored him. Her ankle was killing her, but she was *not* going to let Ian win. He was running now, stumbling across the top of the wall and then jumping off. He zigzagged into a wooded area, howling with laughter and barreling toward her. Amy yanked off her backpack and swung it, clipping him on the arm.

The creep.

"Ow!" he cried out. "That's a fitted Armani shirt!"

The backpack skittered over the ground, spilling out Alistair's overlay—page and scroll clipped together.

"Finders keepers!" Ian shouted, scooping up the overlay and hopping onto a rock outcropping.

"You cheater!" Amy was furious. No way was he going to get away with that. She climbed the rock, matching him step for step until she reached the top. There he turned to her, panting for breath. "Not bad for a Cahill," he said, grinning.

"You—y-y-you—" The words caught in her throat, the way they always did. He was staring at her, his eyes dancing with laughter, making her so knotted up with anger and hatred that she thought she would explode. "C-c-can't—"

But in that moment, something totally weird happened. Maybe it was a flip of his head, a movement in his eyebrow, she couldn't tell. But it was as if someone had suddenly held a painting at a different angle, and what appeared to be a stormy sea transformed into a bright bouquet—a trick of the eye that proved everything was just a matter of perspective. His eyes were not mocking at all. They were inviting her, asking her to laugh along. Suddenly, her rage billowed up and blew off in wisps, like a cloud. "You're . . . a Cahill, too," she replied.

"Touché."

His eyes didn't move a millimeter from hers.

This time she met his gaze. Solidly. This time she didn't feel like apologizing or attacking or running away. She wouldn't have minded if he just stared like that all day.

"Hey, Amy? This hike is rated PG, and we're starving!" Dan shouted. "Not to mention Alistair wants his map!"

Amy felt herself blushing. She turned her eyes away.

"Here," said Ian, handing her the overlay.

Alistair's ripped-out page, which had been attached by a paper clip, was dangling cockeyed. Amy nervously replaced the paper so it was superimposed as before—everything lined up, marking for marking. . . .

Her eye wandered out over the landscape and then back again.

"Oh, my god . . . " she murmured.

"Pardon?" Ian replied.

She checked it again. And again, just to be sure. But it was unmistakable—the shape they noticed earlier on the map. The one they'd been guessing about.

It wasn't palm trees. Or maples.

"Dan!" Amy screamed, leaping down the rock as if her ankle had never been injured. "Everyone! Come quickly!"

She ran back, but the others were on the run, meeting her halfway. Amy took her brother's hand and pulled him up the pathway and up the steep rock. "I love you, Dan, you're a genius," she said.

Dan glared at her. "Did Ian drug you?"

"Look," she said, gesturing over the area. "What do you see?"

"Trees. Rocks. Deer poop." Dan shrugged.

"The rock outcropping. What does it look like?" Amy pressed on.

"Kind of a zigzag?" Ian spoke up.

Suddenly Dan looked as if he'd given himself a wedgie. "It's a W!" he cried out. *"Amy, you found our W!"*

Alistair smiled. "Excellent. X marks the spot on the map—and the spot is a W-shaped rock formation."

Amy took the overlay and began running down the rock ridge. As she got to the edge of the outcropping, she began ripping vines and brush away from the bottom.

"Spread out," Ian commanded. "Look for a cave. A hidden entrance."

The others began poking and tearing, examining the rock. "Look!" Natalie cried out.

Amy ran to her side. She had pulled away a thick bush from the rock wall to reveal a carving of a man. He had a thin, monkeylike face with piercing eyes and a slit for a mouth. "Eww," she said.

"The Bald Rat," Alistair said with awe, running his fingers over the relief. "This is an image of Hideyoshi, in the Japanese style of the period."

"Brilliant," Ian said, rubbing his chin thoughtfully.

"How do we get in?" Dan demanded, his face still buried in the map. "Maybe you've noticed—this big old W is made of *solid rock*. There's got to be some instructions here. . . . "

Amy and the others crowded around Dan. He pointed to the bottom of the overlay. "The letters at the end. Toota. What do they mean?"

T⭕oTA

"Hideyoshi's father was Thomas Cahill — perhaps he taught his son English," Alistair said.

"It's Toyota!" Amy said. "The letters. They spell Toyota without the Y."

"Great, Amy," Dan said. "Our third clue is a buried Sienna minivan."

"I believe she is suggesting that the parchment may be a fake," Ian said.

"Thank you, Mr. and Mrs. Kabra," Dan said, looking closely at the parchment. "But it isn't a fake. Not at all."

He placed the map gently on the ground and pulled a small Swiss Army knife from his pocket. Then, with quick strokes, he began tearing the parchment to shreds.

"*Dan!*" Alistair cried out.

Amy felt her heart stop. "*What are you doing?*"

Dan had the small pocket scissors out now. In a moment, he had carved out all the letters precisely. Handling the thin, fragile cutouts carefully, he arranged them—the big A inside the big O; the two smaller Ts beside each other, upside down within the A; and finally the smaller O in the center:

"It's the symbol for the philosopher's stone," Amy said, astonished.

Dan nodded. "'And by the elements united is entrance granted . . .' I just united the elements."

He was beaming at Amy now. And she knew exactly what was on Dan's mind.

Reaching into her pocket, she pulled out the coin Ian had given her. On it was the same symbol—the philosopher's stone. "Now, let's give that Rat something to eat," she said.

Cautiously, she stuck the coin into the slitted mouth of Hideyoshi.

And the ground began to rumble.

CHAPTER 14

GGRRROOCCCCK...

Ian's knees buckled. The rock outcropping shook the ground, sending a spew of grayish dust that quickly billowed around them.

Shielding his eyes, he spotted Amy standing by the figurine, which was now moving toward her. She was in shock, her backpack on the ground by her feet.

"Get back!" he shouted.

Ian pulled Amy away and threw her to the ground, landing on top of her. Gravel showered over his back, embedding into his hair and landing on the ground like a burst of applause.

His second thought was that the shirt would be ruined. And this was the shock of it — that his first thought had not been about the shirt. Or the coin. Or himself.

It had been about *her*.

But that was not part of the plan. She existed for a purpose. She was a tactic, a stepping stone. She was ...

"Lovely," he said.

Amy was staring up at him, petrified, her eyelashes flecked with dust. Ian took her hand, which was knotted into a fist. "Y-y-you don't have to do that," she whispered.

"Do what?" Ian asked.

"Be sarcastic. Say things like 'lovely.' You saved my life. Th-thank you."

"My duty," he replied. He lowered his head and allowed his lips to brush hers. Just a bit.

The air was slowly clearing, and the noise had stopped. Ian sat up, letting go of Amy's hand. The carving now jutted diagonally outward a few inches from the rock. Where it had been was now a rectangular opening.

A rotten, acrid smell blasted from within.

Alistair was the first to stand, dusting off his carefully pressed hiking pants. "Hideyoshi's hiding place . . . " he said in awe.

Dan and Natalie were right beside him, coughing and shaking off the dust. Dan recoiled as he tried to peek inside. "Dang, someone forgot to flush."

Alistair had found Amy's backpack and was pulling out two battery-operated collapsible Coleman lanterns.

Ian helped Amy to her feet. "Do you have the coin?" he asked gently. "We may need it later, to close up the entrance."

"Po-pock—" Amy tapped her pocket. "I put it in there when the thing s-started to open. . . ."

Alistair handed her a lantern. "You and I will lead, Amy."

As she walked on shaky legs into the cavern, Natalie glared at Ian. He winked at her and walked inside.

Oh, she of little faith.

<hr />

Focus.

All Amy could feel was her lips.

The bluish fluorescent lantern light danced off the crags of a domed cavern, the ammonia smell of animal droppings invaded her nostrils. They were in a cave that most likely hadn't been seen by a human being in half an eon, and her shoes were squishing into a carpet of something she'd rather not see. And all she could feel was the tingle in her lips.

Everything was happening at once. The coin, the hiding place, the . . .

The *what?* What exactly had just happened?

Ian was walking beside her quietly. She was supposed to hate him. She had hated him. But for the life of her, she could no longer remember why. Despite the surroundings, she felt alert, alive, and unbelievably happy.

"Thank you," she said quietly.

"For what?" Ian asked.

"For giving me that coin back in the alleyway in Tokyo," she said. "If you hadn't done that, this whole thing might not have happened."

Ian nodded. "It was one of the Kabra family's most cherished possessions. There were rumors it was the key to a Tomas clue, but my parents didn't believe it. I had to steal it from them." He shuddered. "I will not like to face my father once he's found out."

Amy reached into her pocket and handed him the coin.

"I—I couldn't," Ian said. "I promised."

"We don't need it anymore," Amy said.

"Thank you." Ian took the coin and put it in his pocket. But his eyes were focused upward. "Amy? Do you see something moving up there?"

Amy swung her lantern upward, into a shadow that flitted and danced—and then broke away in a shrieking cloud.

"DUCK!" Dan cried out as a liquid mass of flying bats chittered overhead. They screamed and flapped, their wingtips flicking Amy's hair like rain as she cowered. Then, like smoke through a chimney flue, they exited through the narrow entrance.

"Are you all right?" Ian asked.

Amy nodded. "I hate bats." She sat up, swinging her lantern around, allowing the arc to include his face.

Just to see it.

And that was when Dan yelled again.

"Amy, shine that thing over here!"

It was the coolest thing he had ever seen. Cooler than the lifetime supply of Wii games he'd almost won in his sixth-grade raffle.

Now Alistair and Amy were both racing over, their lanterns illuminating a mammoth pile of objects stacked floor to ceiling. At the top, where the bats had been, a grove of stalactites hung down. They surrounded the pile like an upside-down picket fence holding it in place.

They were swords—a tower of them, arranged neatly in a crisscross pattern. The hilts jutted out, some fancy and jeweled, others dented and dull. They looked like hands, reaching out as if daring someone to pull, which would probably upset the pile like a falling house of cards.

"The Great Sword Hunt of 1588," Alistair murmured. "This is where they were kept."

But Dan was moving past the swords, to the left. The cavern seemed to expand here, wider and deeper, with stacks that seemed to go on into the distance forever. Some of them looked like they'd been thrown there—crowns and helmets, armor, spears, shields, saddles, stirrups. Folded robes winked with inlaid jewels, statues stood covered with dust, and tightly rolled scrolls lay in boxy containers. But one area seemed separate from the others—a shrine, surrounding a strange triangular mirror that hung on the wall in an intricately carved frame.

Around the mirror, huge chests had been stacked in neat piles. They were festooned with jewels and calligraphy, each fastened with a huge padlock.

Dan grabbed one of the locks. It fell apart in his hands, rusted and brittle. As he opened the lid, the others peered in with him.

"As they say in the US provinces . . . " said Natalie, her eyes widening, "bungee!"

"I believe it's 'bingo,'" Alistair said. "By god, these must be the spoils of Hideyoshi—the plunder seized by his forces as they conquered Japan and moved through Korea."

Dan reached in, digging his hands into a trove of gold coins. Next to him, Amy opened another chest. "Plates, chopsticks, cups, bowls, platters—all solid gold!"

"Buddhas!" Ian exclaimed, peering into a third chest. "A collection of miniature golden Buddhas."

"Hideyoshi worshipped gold," Alistair said softly. "According to legend, he even ingested drops of liquid gold each night for its supposed magical properties. . . . "

"We're rich," Ian said. "Again."

Dan smiled.

And by the elements united is entrance granted, the highest to be revealed.

"We're more than rich," he said, letting out a whoop of amazement. "We have discovered the next Cahill clue!"

CHAPTER 15

Alistair did not mind growing old. He did mind being outsmarted by an eleven-year-old nephew.

Gold.

Of course the boy was right. Gold was the "highest element" of alchemy. The alchemical symbol—the "elements united"—was the key to entrance. No doubt this came from the mind of Hideyoshi. Being a son of Thomas Cahill, he would also be a student of alchemy!

Alistair cursed himself inwardly. He should have detected it from the beginning. He could have saved all this trouble, all this danger. All this unnecessary risking of his nephew's and niece's lives.

This was bound to happen.

He was bound to discover a Clue he had already known.

He tried to smile. To the Cahill children, this was all new. They had not been searching for a lifetime as he had. They were dancing now with the Kabras, doing dance moves they called hip-hop, which, when he attempted to join, made his hips hurt.

He kept his eyes on the Kabra boy. Surely the Kabras knew this Clue also. The Lucians had been collecting Clues as long as the Ekats. Perhaps they were just better actors than he.

"Brava!" Ian cried out, lifting Amy in the air. "I knew this cooperation between branches would pay off!"

As he let her down, she allowed her face to brush gently against his.

Alistair felt his blood go cold. The gambit with the Kabras had proved profitable. Without Ian's coin, they could not have found this cavern.

But this was not the sort of alliance he'd imagined.

"I—suggest we leave now," Alistair said. "Perhaps we can discuss what to do next over dinner."

"Not so fast," Ian said. He was walking away from Amy now, intent on the mirror. "Correct me if I'm wrong. It seems to me that whenever you find a clue, you seem to find a lead to the next one."

"Right, Euro-boy," Dan said. "But don't tax your brain. I'm betting the next clue is *not* rock dust."

Ian was eyeing the mirror now. "What do you suppose these letters mean?"

Alistair joined him, shining a light on the triangular mirror frame. Along two sides ran a strange set of symbols.

"Greek to me," Natalie said.

"Guys, I *know* those letters!" Dan exclaimed. "From the inscription we found on the sword in Venice. Remember, Uncle Alistair, when we were looking at those tattoos? I told you there were some letters missing. Here they are!"

"I don't think this is any one tongue," Alistair said, running the letters through his knowledge of thirteen languages. "Perhaps some kind of secret message?"

Natalie began brushing her hair in the mirror with a gold-handled brush. "Mirror, mirror on the wall, who's the richest and smartest and hottest and—"

"That's it, Natalie!" Dan said.

Natalie blushed. "Thank you, I amaze myself sometimes. . . . "

"No! Words on a mirror . . . mirror writing!" Dan quickly pulled out a mechanical pencil and his paperback copy of *Classic All-Time Movie Comedies*. Ripping out a blank sheet in back, he turned the book sideways for support and began copying the letters onto the sheet. Then he held them in the mirror.

It was still nonsense.

Amy cocked her head. "The letters are symmetrical," she said. "The top of each one is a mirror reflection of the bottom. Maybe each letter is a mirrored *half* letter. So if you could see the half letter alone, you'd know what it was?"

"That is the stupidest, most far-fetched thing I've ever heard," Dan said.

Amy grabbed the paper and began erasing half of each letter:

anstkael

Slowly, she began filling in each letter:

ahstkael

"Ahstkael . . . " Amy said. "Isn't that a health food chain in Sweden?"

"Our next clue is in Sweden?" Natalie said eagerly. "I do need a new fur."

Dan tapped his chin. "Um, dudes, these are English? Shouldn't we be trying to make *Japanese* letters? Or Korean?"

"Hideyoshi was the son of Thomas Cahill," Alistair said. "It stands to reason that English was spoken in the home. Hideyoshi would have been fluent. And because the East had not yet opened to the West, words using English letters would have been an unbreakable code."

Dan was scribbling furiously again. He began arranging the letters crazily, in all different combinations.

ALT SHAKE
THE SKALA
SHEA TALK
LAST HAKE
LAKE TASH

"Lake Tash! Is that it?" Natalie shouted.

Dan nodded. "Lake Tash . . ." he said under his breath. "That's Kyrgyzstan . . ."

"Our next clue is in *Kyrgyzstan?*" Natalie said.

"Brilliant," Ian said with a smile. "Well, it was nice to work with you. This time, I'm afraid we will have a distinct advantage."

"But—but—" Amy sputtered.

Alistair watched his niece's expression drop. She would push for the alliance to continue—which would be disastrous. "I will arrange for transportation back into Seoul immediately," he quickly said, pulling his cell phone out of his pocket. "There, we will—"

"Oh, you won't get any reception in here," Ian said, stepping toward the entrance with his sister close behind.

At the cave opening, Natalie grinned, hands in pockets. "In fact, I wouldn't expect much reception for another, oh, five hundred years."

When she pulled out her right hand, she was holding a tranquilizer dart gun.

Alistair scrambled to step in front of his niece and nephew, but Amy pushed him aside. "Natalie . . . ?" she said.

"Guys, this isn't funny," Dan said. He stepped toward them, but Natalie pointed the gun at his face.

"Dan!" Amy screamed, pulling him back.

Ian glanced at Amy. For a moment, she thought she saw a flicker of—something. Doubt? Some kind of indication this was all a big, sadistic joke? Then the look seemed to vanish as quickly as it came. He looked down and pulled the philosopher-stone coin from his pocket. "Oh, by the way, thanks for this."

"How did he get *that*?" Dan blurted, glaring at his sister.

"I-I-" Amy couldn't get the words out. "He—"

"Family heirloom," Ian said. He backed through the opening now, inserting the coin into the mouth of the Bald Rat. "Don't worry. When we win the Cahill challenge, when we amass power that is rightfully ours, maybe we'll come back and pay you a visit. If you're still able to receive us. Meanwhile, my friends, I recommend you conserve your batteries. And your oxygen."

The cave shook. Slowly, the door swung back.

The last thing Alistair saw before the entrance thumped shut was the retreating muzzle of Natalie Kabra's dart gun.

CHAPTER 16

Idiot.

Moron.

Fool.

Amy stared at the door, at the absence of light where Ian Kabra had been standing.

It had all been one big joke. He had wrapped her around his fingers and then yanked her inside out.

How could it have happened? *How could anyone do that?*

Tears made rivulets down her cheeks and fell to the ground, tapping lightly like the flap of moth wings.

Behind her, Alistair and Dan were ignoring her, discussing strategies, trying to figure out how to escape. How to prevent themselves from dying.

Too late, Amy thought. She already knew what *that* felt like.

Slowly, their voices filtered into her brain.

"I am going to search for another exit," Alistair was saying. "Amy, you and Dan look for any weakness in the rock wall. If bats live here, there must be some source of air, some kind of hole."

Amy nodded numbly.

As Alistair's footsteps receded, Dan squatted next to her. "Hey. I want to strangle him, too."

"It was my fault," she said. "I-I believed him. I played right into his trap. . . . "

Dan helped her to her feet and swung the light around, examining every square inch of the wall. The place was pitch-dark, and after a few minutes, Amy already felt like she was growing short of breath.

Alistair's voice echoed toward them from the distance. "No other exits. I just checked the whole W. It goes on much longer than I'd thought. We are totally sealed."

A tomb, Amy thought. *He buried us alive.*

She felt a hand on her shoulder. "I am so sorry, my darling niece," Alistair said gently. "Had I seen you were falling for the boy, I would have done something. It passed over my head, and it should not have."

Amy sighed. "How could I have let him trick me? How could I think that anyone would actually feel . . . "

The words got stuck in the back of her parched mouth.

"I know this will not make anything better," Alistair said, "but you must believe me when I say I know how it feels to be betrayed."

Amy glanced up into Alistair's barely discernible face. "Really?"

Alistair looked as if he were going to say something, then changed his mind. "Think only of this, Amy: Your parents loved you. It was in their eyes, even when you weren't around. You must think of them, and they will be there for you."

"Did you — *know* them?" Amy asked.

"*AGGH!* Gross!" Dan shouted from another part of the cave. "I think I stepped on a bat! Can you guys continue the conversation at a later time — if there is one? If we don't all die and become a banquet for bats?"

Alistair raced away, leaving Amy with a mouthful of questions.

"Dan, you must never, ever give in," Alistair said encouragingly. "A problem is merely a solution waiting to be found. We *will* make it out of here — and I predict we will beat the Kabras to Lake Tash —"

"Dude, we're not going to Lake Tash," Dan said. "I made that up."

Now Alistair was staring at him. "But — the anagram —" Amy said.

Dan sighed, shining his lantern on the sheet where he'd unscrambled the words. "I saw the real answer right away, but I didn't trust them. I threw something out to test them. The real answer is, like, a no-brainer —"

He began scribbling another word on the sheet, but Amy was looking past him, at the odd reflections of lantern light in the mirror.

"Wait!" she blurted out. "The mirror—*who ever heard of a triangular mirror*?"

"Uh, a triangular mirror designer?" Dan said.

"Or an alchemist!" Amy said. "Think, Dan. Alchemy is all about *symbols*. The planets, the elements, everything had its own funny shape!"

"So what was the triangle?" Dan asked.

Amy tried to picture the image on the page. "Air? Gold?"

"Wait . . . wait . . . I can see it . . . " Dan said. "Water! That's it. Wait. No. With the point *down*, it represents water . . . but with the point up, it's fire!"

Dan swung the lantern back in the direction of the mirror now, raising it high above his head.

Just above the mirror, beyond his reach, Amy noticed several greasy-looking, stringy objects. Her stomach turned. They looked like rat tails. "Are they . . . alive?"

Suddenly, Dan glanced toward the ground. He crouched now, scraping something with his fingers. "Charcoal," he said. "It must be leaking from above."

Alistair looked up. "What's up there?"

Choking back nausea, Amy forced herself to follow his glance. To her relief, the hanging tails were way too long to be what she thought they were. They seemed to be just strings, leading into a big crack in the rock.

And she became aware of a very particular smell. "Oh, my god . . . " she said. "Guys, what do you smell right now?"

"Bat turds," Dan said.

"Rotten eggs," Alistair volunteered.

"And that rotten-egg smell," Amy said, "is caused by — ?"

"Chickens?" Dan said.

"Sulphur!" Amy said.

Dan smiled. "Oh, right — I learned that in chem lab last year! I snuck this test tube into Mandy Ripkin's lunch box? With this, like, really loose cork? So when she opened it — "

"Charcoal . . . sulphur," Amy said, wracking her brain for something she'd read in science class. "They go together with some other ingredient to make . . . what is it . . . ?"

"Smelly barbecues?" Dan asked.

Amy suddenly remembered. "Not barbecues, you cheesehead," she said, glancing up into the stringy void. "Gunpowder."

"Uh, you think there's *gunpowder* up there?" Dan said.

"Gunpowder indeed existed in the sixteenth century," Alistair said. "It was developed in China hundreds of years earlier and spread throughout the East."

"Dan, I think these strings are there for a reason," Amy said. "They're fuses!"

"Brilliant, my girl — you are a genius!" Alistair said. "So the mirror has two functions. It points upward, directing our gaze, and it is the symbol for fire. This is *exactly* like Hideyoshi — ever the wily warrior, he developed a failsafe escape for this hideout, in case of sabotage."

"Dan, do you still have the matches from the Thank You Very Much Hotel?" Amy asked.

"You dummy, we can't just blow this thing up!" Dan said. "We could die."

"Gunpowder is not dynamite," Alistair said. "May I remind you, we are surrounded by a lot of schist."

"Watch your language," Dan said.

"Granite schist is extraordinarily dense," Alistair continued. "Blasting through rock in modern times requires far more explosive power than can be provided by gunpowder. Any blast is likely to punch open only a small targeted area. In fact, it is entirely possible the blast will not be strong enough. We will be more than safe with schist."

Alistair was trying to sound reassuring, but Amy could hear the shakiness in his voice. She glanced at her brother. The lantern's shadows on his face made him look like an old man. But even in the distortion of the dim light, she could read his mind.

Do you believe him? his face said.

I'm not so sure, she thought.

Me neither. So we all get crushed instantly under tons of granite, he was thinking.

Or . . . ?

Dan looked away.

Or die a slow, painful death from starvation, was what he didn't want Amy to see. But she felt it.

And the choice, to her, was clear.

"I guess it's the only chance we have to get out and do horrible things to Ian Kabra," Dan said.

Amy smiled, swallowing back a stab of fear that laced through her. "Go for it," she said.

Dan turned to Alistair. "You're taller," he said, handing him the matches.

The old man struck a match and raised it. The flame licked the bottom of one of the strings, flared slightly, surrounded it, and then finally guttered out.

"The fuses are old," Alistair said, tossing the dead match to the ground.

He opened the matchbook to reveal only three matches left. "What happened to the rest of them?"

"Um . . . " Dan said sheepishly.

Amy winced, remembering all the matches he'd wasted on the plaza outside the hotel in Tokyo.

Alistair took a deep breath. "All right, then. Pray."

He lifted another match. It too circled the bottom of the limp string.

FfffffFFFFT!

"Woo-hoo!" Dan cried out, as Alistair lit another string, and another. The flames shot upward into the rock.

"Move!" Alistair cried, grabbing Dan and Amy.

They ran into the cavern, scuttling around the bottom corner of the W.

Boom!

Boom! BOOOOM!

KKKRRRRO-O-O-OK!

An explosion of rock showered down into the cavern, dinging against gold objects, smashing treasure chests. The mirror teetered, finally falling forward and shattering on the ground.

Above them, light poured in through a small hole near the top of the rock wall.

"We did it!" shouted Dan.

All three ran to the spot, stumbling over rock, debris, and broken glass.

CRRRRRACK!

More rocks spat down from above. Amy and Alistair put their arms over their heads, skittering away.

"The rock is cracking!" Dan called out, dragging a wooden box to just below the hole. "Come on!"

Alistair climbed onto the box, reached down for Amy, and lifted her over his head. He was surprisingly strong.

Amy stretched her hands upward, but her fingertips didn't reach.

"One . . . two . . . three . . . alley-oop!" Alistair gave her a thrust upward.

There. "Got it!" she shouted.

Her fingers dug into a broken section of rock. As she pulled herself upward, Alistair put his palms against the soles of her shoes and pushed.

"Hunhhh!" She gasped at the blast of fresh, oxygenated air. Her fingertips grasped hold of a root that had dug itself into the rock. She jammed her elbow into a section of rock and pulled herself clear.

Into the sun. Into the glorious smell of grass and earth.

Splaying herself securely on the surface, she reached her arm back down. "Grab on!"

"Heave . . . *ho!*" Alistair grunted from below.

Amy clasped her fingers around her brother's wrists and pulled. Dan was heavy, and she could only get his torso out—but that was enough. Dan let go and shimmied through the hole.

Quickly, Amy leaned over and called down, "Uncle Alistair! Can you stack any more of those boxes? You'll need to get yourself higher!"

"I'm trying!" he called back.

RRRRRO-O-OMMM!

The entire rock shook. A section of it just to Amy's left collapsed downward. The rumbling seemed to be catching, following the line of a crack in the rock.

"Uncle Alistair!" Dan shouted into the hole. *"Are you all right?"*

Dan put his ear to the hole. Amy could hear Alistair saying something, but the noise of the rumbling drowned out the sound.

Reaching down into the hole, Dan screamed, *"Just grab on! Jump!"*

But there was no response.

Now Dan and Amy were both shouting his name. But the hole, which was only a couple of feet wide, began to split. The entire rock beneath Dan and Amy was breaking. They hurtled forward, down the side of the rock, and finally tumbled to the ground.

As the entire W imploded, left to right in a wave, Amy and Dan leaped away, landing on their knees and covering their heads.

A massive cloud of rock dust billowed upward, blackening the sky. Amy and Dan stared, numb, at the jagged pile of rocks that remained.

Finally, Amy felt the words exit her mouth as if they had a will of their own. "What did he say to you?"

"He said," Dan whispered, "'It's not schist.'"

CHAPTER 17

When Amy ran away behind the tree, Dan knew she was vomiting. And it didn't gross him out at all, because he was doing the same thing.

Alistair had died — inches away from them. Right underneath. He had given them his trust, his money, his advice, his comfort. And finally, his life.

It didn't seem real. He should be behind a bush now, brushing himself off, strolling toward them, his pants somehow still crisply pressed. *Well, that was an adventure.*

But all that Dan could see was dust. Dust and tourists and mounds of rubble and the flashing lights of police vehicles.

And the feeling in the pit of his stomach that he had been through this before. That his whole life had been all about loss. That he had vowed never to get close to grown-ups, because it was so painful to lose them.

And it had happened again.

He was vaguely aware of his sister putting her arm around him. A cop was talking in accented

English, but Dan couldn't put together the meaning.

"His name is . . . " Amy was saying. "*Was . . .* Alistair Oh."

"Age?" the cop said.

The word "sixty-four" came out of Dan's mouth. He didn't know how he knew that, but it occurred to him that Alistair would never be sixty-five. That someday he, Dan, would be older than Alistair would ever be.

"His clothing?" the policeman pressed, which seemed like a colossally stupid question under the circumstances.

"Silk jacket . . . really nice shirt," Dan said. "Um, he always had these white gloves, too. And like a round-ish hat—"

"Bo . . . " Amy said. Her lip was quivering. "Bo . . . "

"Bowler," Dan said quietly.

The cop took notes, but Dan knew he couldn't be treating this as a rescue operation. It was recovery. No one could have survived that collapse.

As he walked away, murmuring a few words of sympathy, Amy stared out over the wreckage. "Dan . . . ?" she said. "Look . . . "

Off to the right, a small entourage had just arrived. They didn't look like the other hikers and park visitors. Most of them were dressed in navy-blue suits with black sunglasses and black shoes, and their ears were plugged with headsets attached to squiggly cords.

In the center was an elderly, thin man with an overcoat draped over his shoulders, a silk ascot tucked into an expensive-looking shirt, and a dark fedora tilted slightly to one side of his head. He moved with a lively step, using a walking stick that was encrusted with jewels.

"That's the guy . . . " Dan said. "The one we saw in Tokyo, outside the subway."

"What's he doing *here*?" Amy asked.

Dan's eyes widened at the sight of someone behind the old man—a person he and Amy were even more familiar with. He had been there at the fire that consumed Grace's house. In Paris and Salzburg. He had never spoken a word, but somehow he was always there.

Amy didn't need to be shown. She saw him, too. "The Man in Black . . . " she muttered, shrinking away.

Keeping low to the ground, she and Dan skittered behind a bush.

"Can you hear what the old man is saying to him?" Amy asked.

Dan stood. He pulled his hood over his head and edged closer, making sure to stay among the ever-growing crowd of gawkers. They were yakking away, too, but as he neared the old man, Dan could see him exchanging bows with the cop who had just spoken to them.

But the Man in Black didn't seem interested in talking. He was walking slowly toward the collapsed rock, his back to Dan.

The old man and the cop were talking now, and Dan could hear snatches of conversation, but it was all in Korean. They didn't say much, and the old man seemed angry and impatient. Finally, after some more bows, the cop left.

With a sharp gesture to his entourage, indicating they should stay put, the old man began striding alone toward the mysterious black-clad stranger.

The two men stood silent, facing the rubble. Dan glanced back at Amy, who had a look of terror on her face, gesturing for him to come back.

But the men were turned away, so he moved closer.

When the old man spoke up, his words were clear. And in English. "My nephew was in there," he said.

The Man in Black moved his head, a slight shift of his mouth registering just a shadow of a reaction — what? Sympathy? Triumph? It was impossible to read.

They seemed to be arguing about something, but Dan could not make out the words.

Then the old man turned, walking briskly back to his cohort. He nodded to no one in particular, but they all fell in step beside him. Together, the whole posse walked away from the site in the direction of the park entrance.

As Dan slipped back toward Amy, he could see the Man in Black approaching the ruins. As he walked through the rubble, he stopped and leaned down.

He seemed to have found something—maybe one of Hideyoshi's relics, Dan thought. Before long, when the rocks were cleared, everyone would know about the treasures. There would be looting, maybe, fights about who the stuff belonged to. All the usual things you saw in the news whenever lots of money was involved.

But for now, the whole thing looked like a big pile of rock. And what the Man in Black was pulling up from the debris didn't belong to Hideyoshi at all.

When Dan saw what it was, a cry snarled in his throat.

It was a bowler hat, crushed and misshapen.

* * *

"Oh, my god, you guys, I thought you were dead!" Nellie screamed. "I heard about what happened. You look terrible!"

Nellie raced toward Amy and Dan, clutching Saladin, as they trudged into the parking lot of Pukhansan National Park. She and Mr. Chung were being interviewed by the police.

Amy's heart went out to Mr. Chung. He was not looking well at all.

Nellie gave Dan and Amy an enthusiastic one-armed hug, squeezing the Mau, who let out a muffled *"Mrrp"* of complaint.

Amy ran her fingers distractedly through Saladin's silver hair. "We escaped. It's a long story, but Alistair . . . "

Her voice drifted off. Behind her, Dan wiped away a tear.

"Yeah, I heard," Nellie said. She put a sympathetic hand on Dan's shoulder. "Come on, dude, let's go back."

On the ride to Uncle Alistair's house, Amy told Nellie what had happened, right down to the sight of the bowler hat. Nellie nodded, listening, and then they both fell quiet for the rest of the trip. Dan kept forming things to say, but they all sounded so stupid. *He was a great man. He really cared about the Cahill family. We'll miss him.*

He realized he didn't really know Uncle Alistair. The old man knew a thousand times more about them than they did about him. He had betrayed them, but in the end he'd saved their lives.

At Alistair's house, birds were chirping in the dogwoods and fluffy white clouds dotted the horizon. It seemed as if nothing had happened. Harold, Alistair's butler, met them at the door, his face drawn and grief-stricken. "I'm so sorry," Amy said.

Dan, Amy, and Nellie removed their shoes and trudged wearily to the kitchen, where Harold had prepared sandwiches. As Nellie ate, Dan pushed his aside. He reached into his pocket and pulled out a wrinkled sheet of paper and a large gold doubloon. "This coin was the last thing he gave me . . ."

"What's on the paper?" Amy asked.

Dan smoothed out the sheet on which he had decoded the last hint.

ALT SHAKE
THE SKALA
SHEA TALK
LAST HAKE
LAKE TASH

ALKAHEST

"That was it?" Amy asked. "*Alkahest* was the clue instead of Lake Tash?"

Dan nodded. "Yeah. The word for philosopher's stone."

"It's an alchemy word," Amy said. "How can it be a clue if it doesn't really exist?"

Dan shrugged, flipping the doubloon in the air. "How should I know? Hideyoshi was an alchemy geek."

The coin came down in his palm, revealing an Egyptian goddess and some cryptic writing.

Amy's eyes widened. "Wait! Oh, my god! Give me that pen!"

She grabbed the pen from Dan and scribbled one word on the paper, below his column:

AL SAKHET

"What's that?" Nellie asked.

Amy was nearly leaping across the table at Dan. "We did a unit on Egypt last year! 'Al' means 'of.' 'Sakhet' is an ancient Egyptian goddess."

Nellie cocked her head. "Serious?"

"The mirror's message . . ." Dan said under his breath. He had to admit, for a dork she could be pretty smart. "Hideyoshi was pointing to the next clue. . . ."

"Nellie," Amy blurted, "do we have enough cash to go to Egypt?"

"Hey, the Kabras may have dumped you, but they never came back to collect the money they gave me," Nellie said. "I say, let's saddle up that camel and ride!"

The room fell into an awkward silence.

Dan shrugged. "It's . . . hard to think about doing this. After what just happened and all. . . ."

"We don't have to think about it now," Nellie said. "Look, if you're not hungry, at least go take a shower. You smell like rotten eggs. Both of you. Dan, you can use Alistair's and Amy can use the one in the guest bathroom."

Dan had to admit that sounded like a good idea. He picked up his napkin and walked into Alistair's bedroom.

Egypt could wait. For a little while.

It smelled nice in there, an Alistair-old-man-ish kind of smell, cologne-y with the scent of fresh laundry. Everything was neat, which was no surprise — the photos lined up on the dresser, the stack of hardcover books on the bedside table, the pillows angled just so — with just a few casual touches, like a pair of gloves thrown on the far side of the bed . . .

A pair of *filthy* white gloves.

Dan detoured away from the bathroom and lifted the gloves. They were caked with dirt and grass and something else. . . .

Charcoal.

"Amy . . . ?" Dan called. *"AMY, COME IN HERE!"*

A cry of happiness welled up but stopped in his throat, as his joy was knocked aside by a realization that made him see black.

Somehow Uncle Alistair was alive.

And he had ditched them again.

EPILOGUE

The old man shut the door of his office and sank into his leather chair. He swung around toward the window, propping his feet on a ledge. They hurt more than usual today. At his age, he disliked long walks.

From below, the muffled sound of traffic wafted upward, the frustrated shouts of motorists, the frenzied calls of sidewalk vendors. A constant reminder of life's true desperate meaning—speed, desire, possession. He was tired of it all. But it wouldn't be long now. The proper path was finally clear.

He flicked on his music system. Richard Strauss's *Death and Transfiguration*. Oddly appropriate, after what happened today.

A stressful day. What was necessary was not always pleasant.

Ah, well. First the death. Now the transfiguration.

He pressed a button on his intercom. "Eun-hee, please contact Mr. McIntyre for me. I have some news for him."

He waited a few seconds but received no response. Strange. Eun-hee had been there when he walked in a few moments ago. She never left her desk in the outer chamber.

"Eun-hee . . . ?" he tried again.

The intercom crackled to life. But the reply was not at all what he expected.

"Hello, Uncle," said a deep, silken voice that sent a knife of fear down his spine. "I trust your trip to the park was pleasant?"

Bae Oh's bony finger began to shake. "Who . . . *who is this*?"

"Why, it's your heir," the voice returned. "What, did I spoil your day? And what a lovely day it was indeed, seeing me die and thus realizing you were spared the trouble of doing the job yourself."

"But . . . " Bae Oh sputtered. "How could you have survived . . . ?"

"A lot of people are wondering this. But I guarantee that when I'm through with you, they won't be asking the same question."

Bae Oh may have been in his ninth decade, but his reflexes were still unmatched. He leaped from his chair and opened the door to the outer chamber.

The room was empty.

The distant sound of footsteps on the outer carpet resounded, then stopped. He was gone.

Bae Oh's knees crumpled. He propped himself on the edge of the desk, feeling his heartbeat race, as behind him, the music swelled.